I0611568

A Picture Perfect Romance

Lynne Sella

WingSpan Press

Copyright © 2015 by Lynne Sella

All rights reserved.

This book is a work of fiction. Names, characters, settings and incidents are either the product of the author's imagination or used fictitiously. Any resemblance to actual events, settings or persons, living or dead, is entirely coincidental.

No part of this book may be reproduced or transmitted in any form or by any means, electronic or mechanical, including photocopying, recording or by any information storage and retrieval system, without written permission from the author, except for the inclusion of brief quotations in reviews.

Published in the United States and the United Kingdom by WingSpan Press, Livermore, CA

The WingSpan name, logo and colophon are the trademarks of WingSpan Publishing.

ISBN 978-1-59594-564-8

First edition 2015

Printed in the United States of America

www.wingspanpress.com

Library of Congress Control Number 2015946687

1 2 3 4 5 6 7 8 9 10

This book is dedicated to Candace Toft. A fellow writer and one of my mentors, her input was invaluable during my final edit and helped make this book a better read.
I will miss our discussions about books and writing immensely.

ACKNOWLEDGEMENTS

This novel is a result of my participation in the Mendocino Coast Writers Conference several years ago. The original idea for this story came to me like a flash of lightning as I stood on the headlands in Mendocino during that conference, waiting for one of the evening programs to begin. Over the years, it has morphed into the novel you hold in your hands today. I would like to thank my original readers, Cindy Nellums and Mary Blackard, who suffered through the first draft and kept me working on it as well as fellow writers Michelle Noonberg and Candace Toft who supported me during the painstaking rewrite. I would also like to thank Sal Glynn, a freelance writer and editor I met at the conference, for reading one of my earlier manuscripts and offering suggestions on how to make it better. Special thanks to local resident, Gladys Hansen, who shared her craft of photo greeting cards with me and to Rachel Miller, former Business Manager of the Mendocino Coast Botanical Gardens, who provided me with information on the gardens and events held there. Thanks also to Debra De Graw from the Mendocino Coast Chamber of Commerce and Mike Kelly, District Superintendent MCCSD, for providing me with information on the water situation in Mendocino as well as Anne Paulson from Opolo Vineyards who provided me with statistics on their wine shipping crates.

A Picture Perfect Romance

CHAPTER 1

B eth Braddock stood in front of the house with her coat wrapped tightly around her, watching men she did not know cart the last of her belongings into a moving van. She was leaving it all behind. The house, the dreams, the memories meant nothing without Craig, and the only person who understood that was his brother, Tony. After the accident, he'd taken care of everything — the mortuary, the realtor, the auctioneer, and the movers. The only decision she had to make was what to do with the rest of her life.

She unfolded the picture she held in her hand and studied the small white house on Mendocino's Main Street. "I think we'll like our new home, Annie." She reached down and stroked the dog's head. "It's right next to the headland trail, and there's a yard big enough for you to run around in." The chocolate lab stood and wagged her tail. "All we have to do is get there."

"Beth, they're almost ready," Tony called as he stepped out the front door and strolled up the sidewalk. "Are you sure you want to go through with this? You can always come north and live with us." Although his hair was lighter, Tony's resemblance to his brother was uncanny.

"I know, but I'm afraid being around you would be like having a picture of Craig in every room. Living some place

1

where I can be anonymous will give me time to sort things out. I'll be fine."

"Well, the offer's there if you change your mind. Now, let's get Annie loaded."

Beth grabbed the dog's collar, and they led her to the back of the enormous moving van. Tony wrapped his arms around her and heaved her into the portable dog kennel that had been placed just inside the door. "Here you go, girl. Now lay down." He stepped backed and let the two men secure the doors.

"Are you ready to go, ma'am?" the taller one asked.

"Just about." She turned to Tony and hugged him. "Thanks for everything. I'll call you when we get there." Then Beth followed the men to the front of the truck.

"I still say this is a bad idea," the other man said as he settled in next to her.

Beth smiled. She knew the owner of the moving company had refused to take her and Annie at first, but Tony can be very persuasive. That and a large bonus had finally convinced the man to agree.

"Sir, that man is on the phone again."

Paul Hayden stepped back from the large, double pane window in his office. Far below him, the intersecting maze of concrete pathways led from one glass tower to the next. Small patches of perfectly manicured lawn and an occasional decorative bush were the only visual stimulation. In the distance, wedges of the coastal mountain range peeked between the buildings.

"What man would that be, Gladys?" he asked, directing his question to the small electronic device on his desk.

"Mr. LaMarr. He says it's urgent."

"What line?"

"Two."

Paul slumped into his black leather chair. He hoped this was good news and things could be finalized. Pinching the bridge of his nose, he picked up the phone. "Davis, have any luck?"

"Mr. Hayden I'm so sorry to trouble you again, but I'm having some difficulty finding the casket you requested. The only oak caskets my suppliers can get are the traditional, rectangular shaped ones with the domed lid and satin interior."

"Mr. LaMarr, my mother led a simple life and insisted on a simple burial. How hard can it be to find a plain wooden casket?"

"Was your mother Jewish?"

"What does that have to do with anything?"

"Well, I can get a wooden casket made of pine with a Star of David carved into it."

Paul closed his eyes and pinched the bridge of his nose again. "No, that won't work. What about a cremation casket?" Dead silence. "Are you there?"

"Uh, yes sir. I don't think that one of those would be appropriate. You see, Mr. Hayden..." Another pause. "They're made of cardboard."

Paul had to agree. While his environmentally correct mother may have thought it ideal, he wasn't burying her in a cardboard box like some unfortunate pet. "Let me do some checking and I'll get back to you." He disconnected and buzzed his secretary.

"Yes, Mr. Hayden?"

"See if you can find a simple oak casket. Nothing fancy, no carving."

"Something like the ones people were using to make wine racks in the '80s?"

"Exactly. One of those would be perfect."

"Right away, sir."

"And Gladys?"

"Yes, Mr. Hayden?"

"For the last time, call me Paul."

"Yes sir — Paul. I'll try."

The software designer looked around his office. Most of his bookshelves were empty, his belongings packed into moving crates and stacked by the door. Between the last minute meetings to bring the other executives at Microsoft up to speed on his current projects and finalizing the arrangements for his mother's funeral, it had taken most of the week to empty out his office. *All that's left to do is to endure the surprise farewell party, pack up the condo, and go home to Mendocino.*

As Paul leaned back in his chair, doubts plagued his mind. What would it be like? Designing software had been the only world he'd known since college, not that he regretted it. His job allowed him to support his mother and keep her beloved bed & breakfast going. But now that she was gone and the place turned a decent profit, he no longer had to work. He could go back to the things he enjoyed. Of most concern to him was whether or not he stilled belonged to the cozy, coastal community. *Mendocino can be such a lonely place.*

A few moments later the intercom buzzed again. "I believe I've located what you're looking for. I'm emailing the page to you now."

"Thanks, Gladys. You're a peach." He swiveled around to his computer and clicked on the most recent message. A picture of an old, stone building popped up on the screen. The salutation identified the place as St. Benedict Monastery in Iowa. Below that was a button labeled "classic caskets." A second click revealed another page displaying a limited assortment of plain wooden caskets, each one hand-crafted by the devout residents. Just what Paul was looking for. Now all he had to do was purchase the one he wanted and get it shipped to the mortuary in Fort Bragg.

He chuckled at the technological savvy of the monks as he added his selection to the shopping cart. Then he provided the necessary information, getting the address off the card Davis LaMarr had given Margaret Hayden several months ago when she began preparing for the end predicted by her doctors. Express delivery would have the casket arriving in two business days. Before leaving the website, Paul clicked on the catalogue request button and had that sent to the mortuary as well. Receiving a thank-you from Brother Timothy via email, he realized just how many people had been affected by his life's work. *Time to go home.*

Beth Braddock wandered out onto the Mendocino Headland and stood at the edge of the sheer cliff. Far below her, waves embossed with foam swirled around the jagged rocks — so hypnotizing, so enthralling. Almost every day she found herself standing in the same spot, the same thought forcing its way into her head. How simple it would be to take just one step — one step to end the pain of loneliness that would not loosen its grip. But each time she felt she was ready, ready to plunge to the rocks below, something stopped her.

Chilled to the bone, she pulled the oversized buffalo-plaid jacket more tightly around her. "Come on, Annie," she called to the dog that had become her constant companion as she headed back to the small white house on Main Street; the house she now called home.

CHAPTER 2

Amy Thompson checked the timer. A few more minutes and the salmon would be done. She did a mental check of the menu. *What have I forgotten?* The salad and dill-cucumber sauce were chilling in the refrigerator, and the sautéed veggies were in a skillet on the stove.

Wine glasses! She hadn't gotten the wine glasses out of the cupboard even though she knew Tom would be bringing some. He carried around bottles of wine like most people carried bottled water.

The timer dinged just as Amy set the glasses on the countertop of the large kitchen island. Although the house had been one of the first built on the headland, the current owner had modernized it just before Amy rented it. Not only did the island almost double the counter space, the Superior built-in stove made cooking a pure joy. She switched off the oven and removed the salmon. The piquant aroma of the lemon and seafood seasonings filled her nostrils as she tore the foil packet open. The pale pink flesh of the fish looked delicious, and after sliding the salmon onto a platter, she arranged the veggies around it. A true gourmet meal, thanks to two semesters of cooking class. She had just returned it to the oven when the doorbell rang. Before she had a chance to move, it rang again.

"For Pete's sake, I'm coming," Amy called as she started for the front door. She could see Tom through the stained-glass window, clutching something to his chest and shifting from one foot to the other.

"Thank goodness," he said as she opened the door. He pushed past her and bustled into the kitchen. He plopped the grocery bag and wine bottle tote he'd been holding onto the island countertop, practically knocking over the glasses in the process. "Thought I was going to drop the wine before you let me in." He took off his brown leather jacket and hung it on the back of a chair. The sleeves of his dress shirt, which he worn open at the neck, were folded under to just below his elbows, revealing a heavy gold watch on one wrist and a gold chain bracelet on the other. "When you said you were fixing salmon, I remembered I had the perfect wine," he said, pulling a pale green bottle of wine out of the neoprene tote.

"I'll bet it's a Chardonnay. I've heard that goes well with fish."

"There's a difference between a wine that goes well with a food and one that enhances it." Tom began opening drawers and rummaging through them. Leaning against the counter with her arms crossed, Amy let her guest continue his impromptu lecture while he searched.

"I think you'll find the flavors of pears, peaches, and citrus of this Pinot Grigio add a tangy contrast to the buttery taste of the salmon." Retrieving a chrome corkscrew from the drawer, he shook his head. "I keep forgetting to pick up a decent wine opener for you." He balanced the kitchen tool atop the bottle and began cranking the handle. "These are almost more trouble than they're worth."

As Tom wrestled with the cork, Amy poked through the grocery bag. "What's this?" she asked pulling out a loaf of bread.

"I picked it up at the deli in Fort Bragg this afternoon. It's loaded with kalamata olives."

"Mmm, sounds yummy. What were you doing in Bragg anyway?"

The cork popped out of the bottle. "Been reading about ice wines," he said as he freed the other bottle from the tote, "and I wanted to try one. The liquor store on Main Street happened to have this one from the Yakima Valley in Washington. It needs to chill while we eat, so it'll be ready in time for dessert."

Amy tucked the bottle into the bottom shelf of the freezer door, opened the refrigerator, and retrieved the salad and dill-cucumber sauce. By the time she had everything ready to serve, including the salmon from the oven, Tom had the wine poured and the bread sliced.

"You've done it again, Amy. This all looks delicious, and I'm starving. My new order of books came in today, so I didn't have time for lunch. What do you say we eat out on the porch? No fog means a beautiful sunset."

"Good idea." She smiled as she dished her plate. Although Tom never seemed to have time for anything other than wine or books, he did have a way of making any occasion, even the smallest event, more memorable. With plates full of food and glasses full of wine, they pushed through the French doors and out onto the porch. As they settled into their chairs, the sun was just beginning to touch the horizon, its reflection rippling on the surface of the ocean as the waves moved toward the shore.

"It doesn't get any better than this," Tom said. "Great food, terrific company, and the best view of a sunset in Mendocino."

Amy had to agree. The huge porch ran along the west and south sides of the first floor with one set of French doors allowing access from the kitchen and another opening out from the living room. Every room had enormous windows, which took advantage of the view in every direction. Upstairs, the master bedroom opened out onto a large balcony that looked down on the bay. Her father had disagreed with her decision to rent rather than buy, but she didn't care. She'd fallen in love with the pale yellow house with its white gingerbread trim the first time she saw it.

As the sun sank lower, the scattered clouds in the blue sky changed from a light copper hue to a deep red, while seagulls flitted across the water. "Do you know who that is?" Tom nodded toward a woman coming off the headland trail. "I've seen her around town a few times."

"I believe her name is Beth, but she's only been in the gift shop once. Most of the time, I just see her walking with her dog."

"Is she visiting someone or does she live here?"

"She moved here a couple months ago. Bought the Hanson place at the end of Main Street."

"Why do you suppose she's here?" Tom asked.

"Your guess is as good as mine. All I know is, she doesn't work and seems to live alone."

"And how do you know so much about her?"

Amy looked at him over her wine glass and then set it down on the table. "Jane. She was delivering the mail the day that woman came into the store, so after she left, Jane filled me in. Apparently, the only mail she sends or receives are her monthly bills."

"What about when she moved in?" Tom asked. "Who showed up to help her?"

"Nobody. A Bekins moving van pulled up, and she and the two movers got out. They opened the back of the van and let the dog out of a carrier. In a couple of hours the van was empty, and she was all moved in. I haven't seen anyone else come around."

"Hmmm." Tom was quiet for a minute or two then he

lifted his wine glass. "Here's to the value of good friend-ship."

"I'll drink to that," Amy said, clinking her glass against his.

After more than two months of sorting and rearrang-ing, Paul Hayden had finally settled himself into his child-hood home, and the surplus items lined the small drive-way of the bed & breakfast. Several people had come to his yard sale, but not many had purchased anything. "Doesn't quite fit with the rest of my décor," was what most of them said, and he had to agree. The chrome and black leather furniture, which had looked great in his Walnut Creek condo, clashed with the more rustic pieces his mother had packed into the family bed & breakfast. It probably would have been easier to unload the stuff before he moved, but everything happened so quickly there really wasn't time. The only thing he kept was the large drafting table she had given him for his college graduation. The rest had to go.

As he wiped the moisture from the cushions for a sec-ond time, Paul noticed a couple strolling along the small picket fence.

"I don't know why you always drag me to these things. I'm not interested in antiques," the man said. Paul didn't recognize him but the woman was the owner of the gift shop around the corner.

"But you need something besides a table and chairs and your computer desk." Her ankle-length skirt, long-sleeved cotton shirt, and loose curly hair reminded him of a younger version of his mother.

"Not really. My chair in the bookstore is quite com-fortable. Besides — hey, will you look at that!" The man's face brightened as he hastened toward the living room set. Paul appreciated his reaction, having felt the same way when he'd found it at Avetex in San Francisco. And judging from the guy's pressed slacks, Armani loafers, and light cashmere sweater, Paul assumed he had an appreciation for high quality when he saw it.

"Are you sure that's the style you want?" The woman frowned as she walked around each piece.

"Just because I live in a rustic building doesn't mean I have to sit on rustic furnishings. I like this stuff."

Time to move in! Paul put on his best salesman face and stepped closer. "Hate to part with all this, but..." he chuckled, "...it just doesn't fit with the décor of the place. Now, of course, there's the sofa, love seat, and recliner." He started toward the small garage that sat at the end of the driveway. "But, I also have a coffee table, end table, and two chrome lamps," he said, tugging open the weathered wooden door.

He'd left those pieces in the garage, afraid their eccentric design would scare off potential customers. The table, a thin sheet of black Lucite, was shaped like a painter's palette and perched on thin chrome legs. The lamps consisted of bulbs hidden under small chrome shades, which were attached to the ends of long poles bent into sweeping arches. Although severe-looking on their own, they complimented the overstuffed leather cushions. As he shifted them into the center of the floor, the woman reached the garage first. "Oh, those are really..."

"Perfect!" The man grabbed one of the lamps and carted it over to the sofa. After positioning it, he stepped back to admire the effect. "Amy, what do you think?"

The woman hesitated a moment and then sidled over to join him. "I don't know, I mean, if you're sure you like it."

"Like it? I love it. This is exactly what I've had in mind.

It'll look great in that spacious room. How much for everything?" he called, as he freed his checkbook from his hip pocket.

"How about $1,500?"

"Are you kidding me?"

"It does seem a little high, Tom." Amy offered Paul a weak smile.

"High? Do you know how much this stuff costs new? Tell you what, I'll give you an extra two hundred, if you'll give me a hand moving it. I just live a few blocks from here."

Talk about easy money, and the guy was still getting a good deal. "Sure. I'll move it back into the garage, and later this afternoon we'll get it over to your place."

"Sounds great. Who do I make the check out to?"

"Mendocino Bed & Breakfast."

Tom tore out the check and handed it over to Paul. "We'll take the lamps and coffee table now."

"Do you want help getting them to your car?"

"Oh, we don't have a vehicle here," Amy said, shaking her head.

"We can carry them, no problem." Tom grabbed the top of the coffee table and tucked it under his arm like a surfboard. "I'll take this if you can manage the lamps, Amy." He grabbed the chrome legs and lumbered out of the driveway.

Amy watched Tom leave and let out a heavy sigh. "He always does this to me." She repositioned her purse and picked up the two lamps. After balancing one over each shoulder, she started after Tom like a rifle bearer of a great white hunter in Africa, carrying the enormous tusks of a bull elephant.

CHAPTER 3

"Set it down here until I figure out how we're going to get it inside." Tom Miller stepped off the curb and into the street, craning his neck to get a better look. Not only was the entrance to his apartment above the bookstore at the top of a steep staircase, the small landing was barely five feet wide. The other pieces of furniture he'd bought at the yard sale had passed through the doorway easily, but the oversized sofa presented more of a challenge. When stood on its end, it was at least a foot taller than the opening, and the four-foot wall, which enclosed the landing, greatly limited any maneuverability.

"I think," Tom began, pointing upward, "we may be able to stand it on end and then slide the bottom through the doorway first."

The man he'd bought it from joined him in the street and looked up at the apartment entrance. "I'm not sure just one of us will be able to stabilize it while the other tugs on the bottom. I mean, one wrong move and the guy on the landing is over the side."

Tom nodded. "We definitely could use a third man. I know, I'll call Amy." He checked his watch. "It's nearly closing time, so she should be able to come." He pulled his cell phone out and dialed her number. "Hey Amy — hang on." He tilted the phone away from his mouth. "What'd you say your name was?"

"Paul."

"That's right!" He turned his attention back to the phone. "Paul and I have everything else moved but the sofa. We're going to need a hand. How quickly can you get here?" After a brief pause he continued. "Surely you can close up a little early. Besides, it's on your way home. I'll even pour you a glass of wine when we're done." Another pause. "Perfect. See you soon."

Tom snapped his phone closed. "No problem. She'll be here in a few minutes."

"Why don't we take the cushions up while we wait?" Paul offered, grabbing two of the large, black leather squares.

"An excellent idea. I'll open up the wine." Tom had been looking forward to his evening glass of wine, sitting on his new furniture and looking through his bay window to the ocean below. Plucking the other two cushions off the sofa, he followed Paul up the stairs.

"If you don't mind putting these somewhere out of the way, I'll get the wine breathing." Tom handed over his load and crossed the open-room apartment to the kitchen area. Reaching into a small stainless steel appliance, he selected a bottle of red wine and began the intricate task of uncorking it.

First, he opened the leather case he kept on top of the special storage unit and used the bronze-colored foil cutter to expose the cork. Then he placed the matching pistol-like wine opener on top of the bottle, plunged the small coil of metal into the cork and removed it with two quick moves of the tool. With the wine properly uncorked, the two men returned to the street, where Amy was waiting for them.

"So, you two managed to get all the furniture moved?" she asked.

"Piece of cake," Tom said. "It was downhill all the way."

She looked from the large piece of furniture to the second story entrance. "Are you sure the three of us can manage this?"

"Absolutely. Paul and I can carry it up and get it into position, and you can guide the bottom of it through the doorway."

"Sounds easy enough. I'll go up first and wait." Amy's short leather boots clunked on the wooden steps as she trotted up to the apartment.

Tom picked up the end of the sofa furthest from the stairs. "Grab hold, Paul, and we'll get this job done."

"Better let me have this end," Paul said, stepping in next to him.

"Why's that?"

"Well, I'm a little taller than you and a good fifty pounds heavier. If this larger sofa should slip, I could probably hold it. You on the other hand..."

"Good point!" Tom set it down and positioned himself at the other end. "Here we go."

The men picked up the sofa and headed for the stairs. Holding the bottom of the large piece of furniture waist high, they began the ascent.

Halfway up, Tom was having a hard time holding on. His arms were shaking and his lower back was beginning to throb. Packing around boxes of books really hadn't prepared him for this. *Moving furniture is best left to the professionals!*

"Tom, are you all right?" Amy called from somewhere above him.

"Can't....talk....now....must....concentrate." With one last push, he reached the landing and set down his end. Then he stepped to the outside edge of the small platform. "Amy, grab hold of that side. We have to lift it to the top of the retaining wall and then stand it on end. Hang on

Paul," he called down the stairs, "just repositioning." The man on the other end of the large piece of furniture muttered something, but Tom was unable to make it out.

Together he and Amy managed to lift the sofa to the top of the short wall and slide it out over the edge as Paul continued up the steps. Just as the wall reached the sofa's mid-line, Paul's end was resting on the landing, and the three of them stood it up.

"Whew, that was harder than it looked!" Tom said, rubbing his back. "Okay Amy, you ready to tug on the bottom?"

"I'll give it a try but shouldn't we turn it so it slides in on its legs?"

"Good idea, but let's pick it up to do that so we don't tear the leather."

The trio lifted the sofa and spun it. Then Tom and Paul leaned it out over the short wall of the landing as Amy began pulling it through the doorway. As soon as it cleared the retaining wall, Paul re-adjusted his grip and helped carry the sofa further into the room.

"I just knew we could get it in here that way," Tom said, following along behind. "Bring it on over here, and we'll see how it looks." He moved toward the large bay windows where the other matching pieces of furniture had already been arranged around a large area rug with geometric designs in black and white. After the sofa had been set into place, Tom positioned one of the odd, bent-pole lights behind it while the other two replaced the large cushions.

"You know," Amy said, walking around the living area, "this really doesn't look too bad, especially with this rug. Where'd you find it?"

Tom crossed his arms in front of his chest, rocked back on his heels, and smiled. "Found it at a yard sale on my last trip through the Anderson Valley."

"You went to a yard sale?" Amy asked.

"Not exactly. They had it draped over the fence right next to the road. Couldn't miss it."

"How did you get it home?" She turned to Paul. "The blue BMW Z3 downstairs is Tom's."

"It took some doing," Tom said, "but I managed to get one end of it stuffed in behind my seat. Had to drive home with the other end sticking out of the passenger-side window. I've kept it rolled up and stashed under the bed."

"So you had no other furniture in here?" Paul asked.

Tom laughed. "Didn't see a need for it. The table is where I eat and read the morning paper. My computer desk doubles as a place to do my bookkeeping."

"Where do you sit to read all those books?" Paul asked, crossing to the massive bookshelf that ran along most of the west wall and almost reached the high ceiling.

"Most of these belong to my rare book collection, so I don't open them very often. The overstuffed chair in my bookstore downstairs is where I usually sit and read. But..." Tom sat down in his new recliner and pushed back. "...I think this is where I'll be reading in the future."

"This is quite a collection, but how do you reach the ones on the top shelves?"

"Oh, I'll show him," Amy offered. She moved to the corner right behind Tom's chair and grabbed hold of a small wooden ladder. "This is the coolest thing — reminds me of those library scenes you see in old movies." She slid the ladder to the center of the bookshelf and climbed part way up. "This and the wine refrigerator were the first things he bought for the place."

"Wine refrigerator?" Paul looked questioningly at Tom.

"The best way to store wine." He ejected himself from the recliner and walked over to the unique appliance in the kitchen area. "This one holds thirty bottles and has dual temperature controls. That way my white wines are chilled to about forty-eight degrees and my red wines stay around fifty-eight degrees. And speaking of wine, I chose a subtle pinot noir for you, Amy. Does that sound good?"

"At this point anything would be great." She climbed down from the rolling ladder and settled into a corner of the sofa. "Wow, this is way more comfortable than it looks, but the leather is kind of chilly."

"That was the only thing I didn't like," Paul said, joining her. "I always thought I might get one of those fluffy, white sheepskin blankets."

"Ooh, that'd be wonderful," Amy said, "wouldn't it Tom?"

"Yeah, sure." Tom retrieved three bulbous wine glasses from the custom-built rack and lined them on the counter. Then he pulled an elongated, egg-shaped aerator from the leather case and began pouring the wine through it. He smiled as each glass received its allotment of the gurgling red liquid. This procedure was the same each time, precisely executed and never rushed. And each time the result was the same — the perfect glass of wine.

He entwined his fingers around the stems of the glasses with the deftness of a seasoned bartender and delivered them to his waiting guests. "Here's to new furniture and the new friend who helped move it in," he said, holding out his glass and clinking it against the others. Then he slowly swirled it, coating the inside with wine and took a sip before the dark fluid stop spinning. Holding it in his mouth for a moment or two, he allowed the pinot noir to permeate every crevice.

"Mmm, this is nice," Amy said, after sipping from her own glass. "We should have this the next time I make my eggplant parmesan."

"I thought you'd like it. It's more mellow than most.

What do you think, Paul?" Tom smiled as he watched the man take his first sip. It was undeniable; he could select a good wine as easily as he could spot a first edition.

"This is very good. I'll have to pick up a bottle of this for myself the next time I'm in Fort Bragg."

Tom chuckled. "You won't find this wine there. It's from a very small winery in the Napa Valley — very exclusive. I'd be happy to pick you a bottle or two the next time I'm there," he said, settling back into the recliner.

"Do you go there often?" Paul took another sip of wine.

"Oh Tom makes about four trips a year to either the Anderson or Napa Valleys. He's gone for a week or longer, looking for new wines or buying up old favorites." She smiled at him and winked. "Someday he'll even let me tag along."

"Someday — maybe."

Paul looked around. "There's something missing here. I can't quite figure out what, but there's definitely something missing."

"Television," Amy said. She finished off her wine and got up. "Tom doesn't have a television." She moved into the kitchen area and set her glass on the counter. "He thinks they're a waste of time and money."

"No kidding. What about keeping up on current events? Or following your favorite team?" Paul set his glass down on the coffee table Tom had packed off from his yard sale earlier that day.

"I receive three different newspapers at the bookstore, and I go online. I don't follow any sports, and my spare time is spent reading. Don't need a television."

Amy crossed back to the sofa and stood behind it. "Give it up, Paul. It's a losing battle. I've tried for over a year to convince him to get one. He won't budge."

"That's too bad, because the wall space between the

two bay windows would be the perfect place for one of those new plasma, flat-screen televisions. Putting it there, you could watch your favorite shows and enjoy the fantastic scenery at the same time." He rose and walked over to the windows. "I have a partial view of the bay from my bedroom window, but this is awesome."

"It's not bad," Amy came around the sofa and stood next to him, "but you should see the view at my place. The house is further out on the headland, so you can gaze at the redwoods trees as well as the ocean. Maybe you'd like to come over sometime and see for yourself."

"That sounds great."

"Okay," Tom said getting up from his chair. "Who wants more wine?"

"Not me. I have to get back to the bed & breakfast and check on the coffee beans in the roaster."

"You roast your own beans?" Amy asked.

"For the espresso machine."

"A real espresso machine?" Amy's eyes widened. "Do you make lattes and cappuccinos with it?"

"You bet. That was one thing I didn't want to do without moving back here, so I bought my own. Thing is, I'm the only one that uses it. Clara — she's my cook — refuses to have anything to do with it. Says she has enough to do without worrying about some newfangled coffee maker."

"That's something I really miss," Amy said. "The closest coffee house is in Fort Bragg, but I can't remember the last time I had a really good vanilla hazelnut latte."

"Well, come on by the bed & breakfast. I'd be happy to make you one anytime."

"Sure you don't want some more wine?" Tom picked up Paul's glass.

"No thanks, I really need to get back." He walked to the door. "Maybe I'll see you soon. Enjoy the furniture."

"I'm sure I will." Tom stepped over and shook Paul's hand. "And thanks for the help getting it here." He closed the door and joined Amy at the windows.

"He seems like a nice guy doesn't he?" she said. "It should be fun getting to know him better."

Tom didn't say anything at first, just stared out at the water. "Yeah, I guess so."

CHAPTER 4

The cinnamon-infused aroma of baking bread enticed Paul Hayden from his slumber. Opening one eye, he tried to focus on the digital clock next to his bed. Half-past five? Although there were a few registered guests, they shouldn't need anything for at least another hour or so.

He rolled over and yanked the blankets over his head, but it didn't help. The smell of the cinnamon rolls permeated the layers of bedding, and images of the giant pinwheels oozing with icing tormented his brain. Finally, he threw back the covers, swung his legs over the side, and got up. It had been the same way growing up; nothing coaxed him out of bed like Clara's baking.

As he pulled on grey sweats and a black T-shirt, Paul thought about the short-statured woman who had become as much a parent as his own mother. Both had been widowed thanks to the Vietnam War, and according to his mother, the two women were brought together by fate. No longer able to support herself in San Francisco, Clara Owens was on her way to Portland, Oregon to live with relatives when her car overheated. Forced to spend the night, she ended up at the Mendocino Bed & Breakfast, and the two women bonded instantly. Clara had sold her car, moved into the small bungalow at the back of the property, and much to Paul's delight, agreed to take over the cooking.

He padded down the steep staircase in his bare feet and into the kitchen. As he hauled the stool over to the stainless steel worktable in the center of the room, Clara pulled a large tray of cinnamon rolls out of the old-fashioned commercial range and set it next to him.

"What got you up so early?" She closed the oven door and tossed the oven mitts onto the shelf above the burners.

"As if you didn't know." Paul reached for a roll.

With the speed of a much younger woman, Clara snatched up a rubber scraper and smacked his hand. "They're too hot, and I haven't put the icing on yet."

Laughing, Paul got up and poured himself a cup of coffee. *Funny how some things never change.* "Fine. I need to grind more coffee beans and fold the load of linens from yesterday. Then can I have one?" He moved in next to Clara. "By the way, I've been meaning to thank you for everything you did for Mom, and for staying on. It wouldn't be the same without you in here rattling the pots and pans."

She craned her neck to look up at him. "I owed Maggie that much." Her eyes filled with tears. "She was a good woman. Now..." she said, swiping them away with a corner of her apron, "...get out of my kitchen, so I can get things done."

"Yes ma'am." He bent down and kissed the top of her head. "Whatever you say."

The fog burned off early, and that suited Beth Braddock just fine. Standing on the headland and basking in the warmth of the morning sun, she took in her surroundings as if for the first time. The waves sparkled in the sunlight, and a crisp breeze blew her hair from her face and numbed her nose. She couldn't remember the last time she'd slept through the night. Often plagued with reoccurring nightmares, sleep usually eluded her, but today she felt rested and relaxed.

As she followed Annie along the trail, Beth marveled at the redwood forest that ran down the mountainside toward the ocean. It was the perfect backdrop for the quaint village, now a mere shadow of its former existence as a bustling harbor. She was glad she'd come and, for the first time in a long time, felt alive.

Amy Thompson tightened her cardigan sweater around her. The walk to work was chilly, but she didn't mind. She wasn't about to pass up an opportunity to be out in the sunshine so early in the morning, especially when she had to be cooped up in the store all day. She let herself in and locked the door behind her. The gift shop didn't open for another hour, and the last thing Amy needed was someone walking in on her while she was focused on the computer.

The new website was a booming success, bringing in way more money than she'd hoped. She was so engrossed in processing the orders and getting them ready to ship, she practically fell out of her chair when the phone rang. With her heart still hammering inside her chest, she managed to answer it before the call transferred to the answering machine.

"Sea Gull Gift Shop."

"Oh, I'm so glad you're open," a bass voice crooned on the other end. "I have a dilemma, and I'm hoping you can help me."

"Uh, I'll try."

"I need to order a birthday present for my sister-in-law, and it needs to be delivered today."

"Today? If I have the item in stock I might be able to get it ready to ship but..."

"That's the beauty of it. She lives right there in Mendocino, so it doesn't need to be shipped — just delivered."

"Oh, that does make it easier, doesn't it? What did you have in mind?" Amy grabbed a new order form from the stack.

"Looking at your online selection, I'm having a hard time deciding. I'd like it to be something special since this is the first birthday she'll be spending alone."

"I see. Well, I have some unusual oil candles. They're made of crystal and burn lamp oil. Are you online right now?"

"Yes I am. Which ones are they?"

"The arch lights. They come in three different designs, and I have several colors of oil to choose from."

"Oh, those are very nice. How about the diamond-shaped one with green oil?"

"Okay." Amy jotted down the item number. "Apple green or a deeper emerald green?"

"Let's go with the darker green. Can you wrap it and include a card?"

"Sure. How would you like it signed?"

"All our love, Tony and Steve."

Amy's hand stopped, her pen poised in mid-air. *Tony and Steve?* "Uh, and her name and address?"

"Beth Braddock. Four hundred Main Street."

"No kidding."

"Oh, do you know her?"

"Not really, but I've seen her around town with her dog."

"That would be Annie. Friendly enough but a bit set in her ways."

"Really? I never would have guessed that about your sister-in-law."

The man on the other end of the line laughed. "I was talking about the dog. You can't make Annie do anything she doesn't want to. Beth, on the other hand..." There was a pause. "I'm not sure she knows what she wants. Not yet. If only she could find someone to spend time with, someone to be a friend..." Another pause. "So then, we're all set and you'll deliver it today?"

"I'll take it over as soon as my clerk shows up. The only other thing I need is your name and credit card number."

"Of course. Tony Braddock, and my card number is..."

After hanging up, Amy located the oil candle the man wanted and set it and a bottle of lamp oil on the counter. She'd have Sandy wrap them as soon as she got there. For the moment, Amy had four other orders that needed to be processed. She was almost done when her clerk knocked on the door.

"Morning, Boss Lady," she said as Amy let her in. "Isn't the sun just glorious this morning? I felt like I could've run forever. In fact, I stayed out so long I was almost late." She ran her fingers through her long, blond hair, which was still damp from her shower. Then she gathered it all up and secured it into a ponytail at the back of her head. Amy grimaced at the row of earrings adorning each ear, grateful the only other visible piercing was the tiny diamond stud that penetrated her left nostril. At least the yellow miniskirt Sandy wore accentuated her toned legs perfectly. Amy had always admired smooth, muscular legs but wasn't willing to put in the hours of exercise they required. "Before you do anything else, I need you to wrap the arch light on the counter and select a birthday card from the rack, but nothing mushy."

"Gotcha," Sandy said as she pulled off her oversized sweatshirt with a College of the Redwoods logo and stashed it under the counter.

As the shipping labels printed, Amy packed the last item in popcorn, placed a small card explaining her environmentally-friendly packing material on top, and taped the box shut. With the labels stuck in place, the orders were ready to go; she'd send them with Sandy to the post office later. Then Amy emailed each customer a shipping notification.

"I'll be right back. I have to make this delivery." Amy placed the four packages on the counter and filled out the birthday card Sandy had left next to the wrapped arch light. "While I'm gone, will you please make some more popcorn? I used up most of what we had left on these orders."

"Sure thing, Boss Lady."

Amy cringed and wished her clerk would just call her by her first name. Shaking her head, she slid the gift and its card into a bag and headed out the door.

What are you barking at? Beth Braddock had never heard Annie carry on so. She rinsed the last dish and propped it in the drainer. Drying her hands on a kitchen towel, she walked to the front door and opened it. Annie had taken position in front of the gate and was barking at a rather nervous-looking woman standing on the other side. She smiled when she spotted Beth.

"Good morning," she called, as the dog continued to bark. "I have something for you." She raised her hand, which clutched the handles of a large red bag.

"Annie, stop that. Come here, girl." Beth patted the side of her leg, and the chocolate lab left her post. When the dog joined her on the porch, Beth ushered her inside and closed the door. Then she started toward the gate, but before she could reach it, the woman undid the latch and hurried up the sidewalk. "You're Beth Braddock, aren't you?"

"How did you...?"

"And it's your birthday, too!"

Beth took a step back as her uninvited guest got closer. "But how did you...?"

"This is for you." The woman thrust the bag at her. "Your brother-in-law called me — I own the Sea Gull Gift Shop — and asked me to deliver this."

"Uh, thank you." Tentatively, Beth reached out and took the bag.

"I'm Amy Thompson, by the way, and we're sort of neighbors. I live in that yellow house," she said, pointing toward the headland.

"I see." Beth switched the bag from one hand to the other.

"I've lived here almost five years, now. Such an interesting place, don't you think? Moved here after a messy divorce, decided to stay for a while, and bought the shop. How about you? What brings you to Mendocino?"

Beth took another step back. "I'm sorry, but I need to go. I have something cooking on the stove," she lied.

The woman's smile faltered just a little. "Oh, of course."

"Thanks again for bringing this by."

"Glad to do it. I hope you like it." Amy started for the gate but stopped. "Come by the shop, and I'll treat you to a coffee at a nearby bed & breakfast. Best lattes in town." She stepped through the opening and closed the gate behind her. One last wave and she was gone.

Beth climbed the steps, opened the door, and was nearly bowled over by Annie. The dog let out three or four good barks before realizing there was no one to bark at. She patrolled up and down the fence a couple of times and then curled up in her favorite spot at the bottom of the stairs. "Try to behave yourself, you goofy dog," Beth scolded and went inside.

It was inconceivable that she'd been living in Mendocino for over two months. And for Tony to remember her birthday was very touching. With an excitement that seemed unfamiliar, she removed the gift from the bag, set it on the kitchen table, and dropped the bag on the floor. Then she grabbed the phone and punched in Tony's number.

"Braddock."

"Hi Tony, it's Beth."

"Hello there, Birthday Girl. I'm so glad you called."

"I just wanted to thank you for the present."

"Do you like it?"

"I don't know; I haven't opened it yet."

Tony chuckled. "Only you would thank someone for something you haven't seen. Go ahead and open it."

"Now?"

"Yes, now. I want to know if you like it."

"Well, okay. Hang on a second." Beth laid the phone on the table. Then she tore the paper off the rectangular box, opened the flap, and pulled out a cube of Styrofoam. Carefully she pulled it apart to reveal a clear glass arch with a diamond-shaped receptacle hanging from the top. Beth set it down on the table and picked up the phone. "It's beautiful, Tony."

"Is the color of oil okay?"

"Oil?" Beth looked into the empty box.

"Yeah, there should be a bottle of dark green oil to put in the thing."

Beth picked up the bag and peered inside. A card was all she found. "I checked the box and the bag — no oil."

"Well, for the love of — I'll call that woman again and find out what happened."

"You're busy, I can do it."

"But you shouldn't have to be the one handling it. It's your birthday present."

"Really, I don't mind." It would give her a chance to apologize to the woman for ending their conversation so abruptly. She wasn't even sure why she'd done it. *Maybe her enthusiasm made me nervous or maybe it was all the questions she asked. Maybe…*

"Are you there?"

"Sorry. What were you saying?"

"That it probably would be better if you did check on the oil. I have a staff meeting in a few minutes, followed by an appointment with a client at a local restaurant. I'm not even sure when I'd get a chance to call."

"I told you you were busy. I'll go to the shop right now."

"Then I'll leave it to you. So long, Beautiful."

"Bye." Beth laughed as she hung up the phone. *What a charmer, too bad he's gay.* An opinion with which she was certain his life partner, Steve, would disagree.

Leaving the arch candle on the table, she grabbed her jacket off the back of the bedroom door and went outside. "Come on, Annie. We have an errand to run." Happy to be included, the dog frolicked around Beth's legs as she strolled up Main Street toward Lansing.

Two blocks north, the shop wasn't hard to find on Ukiah Street. Certain she'd been there at least one time before, Beth left Annie sitting by the door and went inside. The quaint little shop had a rather eclectic selection of jewelry, organic beauty products, and interesting trinkets as well as a photo-developing machine in a back corner. The pungent smell of scented candles mingled with the warm aroma of freshly popped popcorn. She spotted the woman who had delivered her present standing behind the counter. Nearby, a younger woman with long blond hair was straightening photo cards in a wire rack.

"Are you sure you don't want to order more?" she asked. "There are only a few left."

"Not really. They cost too much and the pictures aren't that good. I may have some more to put out." The woman disappeared momentarily as she ducked behind the counter, but Beth could hear her rummaging around. "I wish I could find another source for these, but right now I don't know of any other photographers who are doing them. Here." She reappeared and handed over a small bundle of cards and then slid a stack of packages across the countertop. "When you're done with that, I'd like you take these to the post office."

"Gotcha. Need anything else while I'm gone?"

"No, that should do it."

As soon as the girl left, Beth approached the counter. "Excuse me."

"Can I..." The woman smiled. "Oh, I didn't expect to see you so soon."

"I'm sorry, but I forgot your name." Beth felt the color of her face deepen.

"Amy. I'm so glad you came by. Did you like your gift?"

"Oh yes, it's lovely. But..." Beth hesitated.

"It wasn't broken was it?"

"Oh no. But when I called my brother-in-law..."

"Tony, right?"

"Yes. When I called Tony, he said something about oil being included."

"The oil!" Amy smacked her forehead with one of her hands. "It wasn't in the bag?"

"I didn't find anything other than the card."

Her hands dropped to her sides. "Sandy!"

"I beg your pardon?"

"My clerk was supposed to wrap it and put it with the candle. I'm so sorry. Let me grab it for you." Amy slipped out from behind the counter and vanished through a door at the back of the shop. While she waited, Beth looked at the cards in the display. They were just blank greeting cards with photos of the Mendocino area glued to the front. She had to agree; who would want to buy such poor quality pictures?

"Here we are," Amy called as she bustled through the door. By the time she reached the front of the shop, Beth had replaced the cards in the rack. "This is the one Tony ordered," she said, placing the bottle of dark green oil on the counter, "and this one's on me." The second bottle of oil was a deep aquamarine and reminded Beth of the geothermal pools she'd encountered at a volcanic park when she was a child.

"You don't have to do that."

"Oh, but I'd like to. Besides it's always nice to have a choice, don't you think?" Amy rolled each bottle in tissue paper and slipped them into a smaller version of the red gift bag she'd delivered earlier. "Is there anything else I can help you with? I'd take you for that latte but Sandy's not here to watch the shop."

"Oh, I didn't come..." Beth stammered as she picked up the bag. "I mean..." She glanced toward the door.

Amy smiled. "No need to explain. Perhaps another time."

"Yes, another time." Beth nodded and returned the smile. "That would be nice." She took a few steps and turned back. "Bye, and thanks again." Then she hurried through the door. "Come on, Annie. Let's go home."

CHAPTER 5

A nother good night's sleep followed by a morning without a wisp of fog had Beth Braddock practically skipping along the headland trail. Invigorated by her outing, she prolonged her walk by strolling up and down the narrow streets, looking at the historical storefronts and countless vibrant flowers that were beginning to bloom. *How perfect the small town seems. Picture perfect. Photo perfect?*

She stopped at the crest of the small hill on Little Lake Street and slowly turned. She'd seen it all before — the towering redwood trees, the white-topped waves of the ocean, the sprawling carpet of vegetation, the dollhouse look of the buildings — but this time it was through a photographer's eyes. The colors and composition were practically textbook. Only a blind man could take bad pictures of Mendocino. *Perhaps that explains the photo cards in the gift shop.* She giggled.

Her mind racing, she started down the hill toward home. She had everything she needed; wide angle lenses, telephoto lenses, magnifying lenses for close-ups. Her pace quickened. Two different tripods, an autowind. *Faster!* Craig had always said she was a topnotch photographer. In fact, he bought her that expensive camera for their first anniversary and when she opened it...

Beth stopped so abruptly Annie ran into the back of

her legs, almost knocking her down. *My camera! Do I even still have it?* All of that stuff had been in the hall closet, but hadn't she told Tony to get rid of it when they were cleaning out the house? She couldn't remember. Couldn't remember much of anything from the time of the accident until she moved to Mendocino.

She took off at a dead run, her loyal companion giving chase. She had to find it; it had to be there. Beth rounded the corner onto Heeser Drive, her arms flailing to help keep her balance. By the time she reached the front gate, she was gasping for breath. She flew up the stairs and burst through the front door, leaving Annie on the porch. *Where can it be?*

She jerked open the front closet door and quickly scanned the shelf. Then she shoved the coats and jackets first one way and then the other, trying to get an unobstructed view of the floor. No camera. Beth repeated the same procedure in the bedroom closet with the same results. *Now what?*

The small one-bedroom house didn't have much storage. Neither the pantry in the kitchen nor the cabinet in the bathroom that served as a linen closet was big enough to hold the camera with all its accessories. Beth flopped down on the bed and closed her eyes. She did a mental check of all the things she'd brought with her. The few pieces of furniture and appliances, boxes packed with clothes, linens, pots and pans, Annie's bed, and what few tools she needed to maintain the large yard. Everything had fit in the house except the tools, and they got put in the... *The garage!* It was really more like a huge shed, and she hadn't been inside other than to toss in the boxes she'd emptied while unpacking.

She leapt off the bed, hurried out the back door and was immediately joined by Annie. Together they trotted down the narrow sidewalk to the small white building at the back of the property. Beth slid over the bolt-like latch, flipped the light switch, and stepped inside. The dim glow from the bare bulb hanging from the ceiling didn't make much difference, and the damp smell of mold and mildew penetrated her nostrils. A tower of discarded boxes filled most of the old dilapidated shed, obscuring from view whatever else might be in there. Methodically, she began nesting them until a double row of boxes lined one side of the room.

"I didn't realize there were so many boxes of stuff still in here. Do you think my camera's in one of them, Girl?"

The chocolate lab, who had found a place to lie down and watch, raised her head and offered a soft whine.

"You're right. There's only one way to find out. At least they're labeled." Beth wasn't sure who had done it, but each had been marked with the word "garage" followed by a brief listing of the contents. Most held books. Clay pots and potting supplies filled a couple, and one contained a large kettle for canning and some jars but no camera. Wondering why she'd even started all this nonsense in the first place, she uncovered the last box. It was bigger than the rest, but she couldn't see a label anywhere until she rolled it over. Then she squealed.

The sound sent Annie to her feet. "Oh sorry, girl. But look, I found it." Beth squatted next to the large box, wrapped her arms around it, and picked it up. It wasn't heavy just awkward to hold on to. Panting, she got it up the back steps and into the kitchen. Squatting again, she set the box on the floor, grabbed a knife from the drawer, and sliced through the tape that held it closed. "This is like getting another birthday present," she told Annie, who had found another vantage point where she could lie down and watch.

Slowly Beth opened the flaps and peered inside. The contents had been covered by a sheet of newsprint and a note, written in familiar handwriting, lay on top.

Dearest Beth,

You told me to get rid of this stuff but I couldn't bring myself to do it. Some day, when the sadness leaves your heart, you may want to do those things that once brought you joy. Please don't be angry with me. I only want you to be happy.

All my love,

Tony

P.S. Your manuscripts are in here, too.

"My manuscripts?" Peeling back the newspaper, she instantly recognized the Christmas gift box decorated with a collage of Santas but wasn't ready to deal with the feelings and memories that were hidden inside. Instead, she carried the gift box to the front closet and stashed it on the shelf, next to a small chest filled with pictures, scrapbooks, and other keepsakes. Then she returned to the kitchen. "Now, let's see what's in here?" she said as she sat cross-legged next to the box of photo equipment.

A large, black leather carrying case was the first thing to come out. When she unzipped it, Beth was relieved to find her camera. Also in the case were several lenses, her autowind, and the mini-tripod. After popping the camera's protective cover off, she looked through the lens, "Say cheese, Annie," and pushed the shutter button, but nothing happened. Turning it around, she spied the small compartment that held the battery and popped it open. Empty. "At least I took the old one out."

Turning her attention back to the box, she dug out the larger tripod, a small light table for examining negatives, and a red suitcase. A carrying case for roller skates, Beth had used it to hold her proofs and thousands of negatives she'd accumulated over the years.

Anxious to get started, she tucked everything but her camera and the black leather bag into the front closet and tossed the empty box back into the shed. Then she dug out the owner's manual and located the type and size of battery she needed. "I'll pick up a new one when we get some film," she said, jotting down the information on a piece of paper.

Beth grabbed her purse and started for the door, but when her stomach growled, she remembered she hadn't eaten breakfast. Seeing Annie next her empty dishes made her realize she wasn't the only one feeling hungry. "Okay," she said putting her purse down, "we'll eat first. Then we'll go."

With the last package ready to be mailed, Amy Thompson had thirty minutes before the shop opened. "Just enough time to get a latte," she said to herself as she clicked off the computer monitor and grabbed her sweater. Maybe Paul would have time to sit and visit.

She strolled down Lansing Street, letting the sun warm her face. As soon as she stepped through the door of the bed & breakfast, she caught a whiff of something sweet and buttery, and the clink of utensils against china suggested breakfast was in full swing. She tiptoed across the tiny lobby and peered into the dining room.

Carrying a coffee pot and a pitcher of water, Paul moved from table to table contributing to the conversations in addition to refilling cups and glasses. A man who truly loved his work. Not wanting to interrupt, she started to leave.

"Amy, don't go," Paul called, having spotted her. "Come in, come in."

"You're busy," she said turning back toward the dining room. "I'll come back later."

"Nonsense. Here," he said, depositing the two containers on an empty table, "sit down and I'll get your coffee." He ushered her to a small table just inside the door and then disappeared into the kitchen. Seconds later he returned with a small plate and a fork, which he placed in front of her. "Have a piece of Clara's coffeecake. She baked it fresh this morning."

Amy recognized the aroma coming from the deep yellow cake topped with a thick layer of brown sugar crumbles. "Mmm, this looks good," she said as she plunged the fork into a corner of it.

"Almost as good as her cinnamon rolls," Paul said, smiling at her. Then he stepped to the espresso machine at the back of the dining room and began making her vanilla hazelnut latte.

Amy's lips slid the first bite of coffee cake off the fork, and she rolled her eyes as it melted in her mouth. Never had she tasted anything so delicious; unfortunately her waistline would probably divulge every bite. Listening to the hiss and puff of the espresso machine and smelling the coffee, she knew she could definitely get used to hanging out there.

By the time Paul set her latte in front of her, most of the guests were gone right along with her coffee cake. "I see you didn't waste any time," he teased, sitting across from her.

She gave him her best coy smile. "Couldn't help myself. It's so yummy, just like your lattes." She picked up the heavy white mug and took a sip. "Perfect, as always."

"Uh," Paul chuckled and pointed toward her face, "you have a little foam on your..."

Amy quickly brushed at her lips with her hand.

"Actually, it's on the tip of your..."

She crossed her eyes and looked. Sure enough, a large dollop of foam decorated the end of her nose. A wave of heat traveled from her chin to the top of her head.

Paul laughed and reached across the table with the towel he'd had on his shoulder. "I'm sorry but that was quite a face." He dabbed at Amy's nose. "There, that's better."

"Thanks," she mumbled, avoiding his gaze and smoothing out the foam with her fork.

"Guess I piled it too high. I'll have to remember that in the future." He winked at her.

"Are you going to clear those tables or are you taking the rest of the morning off?" A woman, short on stature but long on girth and wearing a white apron, stood in the doorway with her hands on her hips. Her straight white hair was cut short, giving her the appearance of an old pixie.

"Be right there, Clara," Paul said without turning around. Leaning closer to Amy, he whispered, "She has this thing about getting the dining room cleaned up by nine o'clock."

"What time is it?" Amy asked.

Paul checked his watch. "Five minutes after."

"Oh my gosh, I'm late." She jumped up, pulled a five-dollar bill out of her sweater pocket and laid it on the table.

"What about your coffee?" he asked as he got to his feet.

"Can I get it to go?"

"You bet. Hang on a sec." He grabbed a large, white paper cup off a tall stack next to the espresso machine and dumped her drink into it. Then he popped on a plastic lid. "There you are," he said, handing it over.

Amy thanked him and hustled out the door. As she rounded the corner, she spotted Sandy peering into the shop, her hands cupped around her eyes. "Yoo-hoo," she called, waving her hand in the air. "Be right there."

Sandy returned the wave. "Hiya, Boss Lady. I was wondering where you were."

She held up her cup. "I finished the online orders and decided to get a latte."

"Gee, seems like you need one almost every day. Not that I blame you; he's hot."

"You mean Paul?" Amy slid the key into the lock. "I suppose he is good-looking."

"Definitely eye candy, for an older guy, that is."

Eye candy? "But really, I only go there for the lattes." She pushed the door open. "You should try one; they're delicious."

"That's your story, and you're sticking to it. I get that." Sandy flitted toward the backroom.

Amy pulled the key out of the lock, flipped the sign from closed to open, and shut the door. *How absurd, I hardly know the man.* Besides, she was fairly certain he wasn't her type. She took off her sweater and stashed it under the counter. At least she didn't think he was.

CHAPTER 6

"Not this time, Girl," Beth Braddock said, pulling the gate closed behind her and confining the dog to the yard. "I need to focus on my photography, not worry about you." With a fresh battery and new roll of film loaded into her camera, she was ready to begin her new venture. She crossed the street and followed the trail out onto the headland. Not used to being left behind, Annie paced back and forth, barking until Beth disappeared from view as she made her way along one of the narrow trails down to a small beach on the north side of the bay.

Low tide allowed her to clamber over the wet, slimy rocks to where ceaseless waves had worn a large arch through an outcropping of sheer cliff. Crouching down, Beth used the texture of the weathered rock to frame the ocean beyond. Then she followed an alternate route up the cliffside and paused just before reaching the top. Peering over the ledge, she realized Annie had curled up in her favorite spot and was probably asleep, so Beth continued north on the headland trail.

Eventually she found herself way out on Heeser Drive, taking pictures of the coastline. Some shots she took looking down from the cliff tops and others were from the beach looking up along the shore. The last picture she took was of a group of sea lions sunbathing on a small island of rock. With only a few exposures left on the roll, she decided to take a couple of the headland across the small bay and some looking back at Mendocino. Nothing spectacular, but pictures that people would easily recognize. Then she headed back to her house.

As soon as Beth opened the gate, she was ambushed by Annie. "Get down," Beth scolded. "What's gotten into you?" She patted the old dog's head, went inside, and loaded another roll of film in her camera. Emerging a few minutes later, she found Annie barricading the gate. "What are you up to?" Beth asked her. Annie did not move. "You have to stay here. I'll be back in a little while, now go lie down. Go on, lie down," she repeated. Reluctantly Annie moved away from the gate and lay down at the base of the steps. "Good girl," Beth said, latching the gate behind her.

Wandering the streets of the tiny town, she took pictures of the quaint storefronts as well as the older homes that were being used as bed & breakfasts, their weathered planks a sharp contrast to their cheery signs. When she finished off the second roll, she started for home. Rounding the corner onto Main Street, she was astounded to see Annie charging toward her. The dog's mouth was agape, and her tongue and ears flailed about. "Annie, what are you doing here?" Beth demanded, reaching down and grabbing her collar. "How in the world did you get out of the yard?" A wagging tail was Annie's only reply.

"Now that I don't have to check on you, we might as well turn in this film." Beth spun around and, going back the way she'd come, soon arrived at the gift shop. "Wait here," she told her companion and went inside. Standing at the small counter in front of the photo-developing machine, she rewound the film in her camera, dropped both rolls into an envelope, and slid it through the slot. Then she stepped over to where the clerk was thumbing through a magazine. "Excuse me, do you sell stationery items?"

The young woman flipped shut the *Cosmopolitan* she'd been reading. "I'm sorry. What did you say?" she asked, speaking as though she had a large ice cube in her mouth. Beth had to suppress a smile when she realized that ears weren't the only body part that the girl had gotten pierced.

"Stationery. Do you sell stationery?"

"No, but I think there's stuff like that at the Seaside Art Supply over on Main Street." She picked up the magazine again and waited.

"Okay, thanks."

Beth traveled down Lansing toward Main Street once more. Inside the small store, she found the rack with card-making supplies almost immediately. On the backside were some eggshell-colored card stock and matching envelopes. Beth picked up two packages. That would give her sixteen different samples that she could show to the owner of the gift shop. Making one more pass around the rack, she spotted the clear sleeves for individual cards. The last thing she needed was some way to attach the photos. Looking at all the options, she settled for a small jar of rubber cement. After paying for her purchases, she and Annie headed home.

A morning with no customers didn't bother Tom Miller. It was, after all, the tail end of the off-season. Besides, it allowed him to inventory the wine stored in the basement and vacuum the books on the shelves. That done, he poured himself another cup of coffee and sat down at the new computer that he'd just installed behind the counter.

Double-clicking an icon on his desktop, a one-page advertisement popped up on the screen. One of his better graphic creations, he used it repeatedly for the bimonthly readings he hosted at the bookstore. After changing the date and the name of one presenter, he minimized the document and opened his email. The poet he'd contacted earlier had yet to commit.

Sipping his coffee while scanning the names as they appeared from cyberspace, he practically choked when he spotted her name. Debra Osborn. Deborah had shorted the spelling of her name, claiming she could never "bor" anyone. She had, however, aggravated the hell out of Tom more than once. And here she was, doing it again.

With the anxiety typically saved for a root canal, Tom clicked open the message and began to read it aloud. "Dearest Tom, I know now what a big mistake it was to let you go."

"Let me go?" Tom queried the computer. "I'm the one that gave you the boot." He read on.

"These past few years, I've done a lot of soul-searching and realize you are the one I'm supposed to grow old with. And I'm sure you feel the same way. I just hope I haven't waited too long."

"Oh for the love of..." Tom got up. Craving a bold Cabernet, he topped off his cup with coffee instead and settled into the comfy chair in a corner of the bookstore. The woman was a nutcase, and one of the reasons Tom had left Los Angeles. Her controlling clinginess had turned him into a devout bachelor. She'd probably located the bookstore's website via the internet, but why now? *And why me?* Certain De-bor-ah wouldn't, in the words of his favorite poet, "go gently into that goodnight," maybe his old friend and known member of the mafia, Carmine Scaglione, could help him. However, his solution might be more permanent than Tom was looking for.

Returning to the computer, he decided the best course of action was to do nothing. He deleted the message just as his first customer of the day entered the bookstore. She looked familiar but the name eluded him.

"Can I help you?" Tom asked, stepping around the counter.

"I'm looking for a map or a book of local points of interest."

"I have both." He led her over to the magazine display. "This is a map of all the nearby state parks," he said, handing one to her. "And this travel guide," he rested his hand on a small green book, "covers places along the coast from Gualala to Leggett. Are you on vacation?"

She smiled at him. "No, I moved here a few months ago. Beth Braddock." She held out her hand.

"Tom Miller." The firmness of her grip surprised him. "Oh yeah, you're the one that arrived in the moving van, aren't you?"

Frowning, the woman pulled her hand away. "How do you know that?"

"Don't be nervous." He waved her off. "My friend, Amy, lives not far from you and watched you move in. Where's your dog?"

Her smile returned. "She's outside, waiting."

"Is she well-behaved?"

"I guess so."

"Then bring her in. Can't browse through a bookstore properly if you're worried about a dog." Tom walked to the door and held it open. "Come on, I've got a place where you can get comfortable for a while." The large brown dog, hobbled into the store. "Something wrong with it?" he asked.

Beth laughed as she bent down and scratched the dog's head. "She got a little more exercise than usual."

"I see. Well, come over here, Girl." Tom slapped the side of his leg a couple of times as he moved to the braided rug in front of his comfy chair. "Lie down," he said, snapping his fingers and pointing to the floor. The dog looked up at him, walked in a circle three times, and flopped down.

"How did you do that? The only person who could make her obey like that was my husband."

"Grew up with seven brothers and sisters and a father who loved to hunt. We always had plenty of dogs around, though I never much cared for them. You aren't one of those overprotective dog owners, are you?"

"Actually, I'm more of a cat person. Annie was Craig's hunting dog, but I couldn't bear to get rid of her." Beth smiled at her canine companion. "In fact, we've become good friends."

"She doesn't seem that old? Doesn't he hunt anymore?"

The woman's face lost all expression as she took a step back and sat on the polished wooden bench near the magazine rack.

"You okay?" Tom asked, stepping toward her.

She held up her hand. "Just a little dizzy." She gripped the seat with both hands. "I'll be fine in a second."

"I'll get you a glass of water." He started for the back of the bookstore.

"No, really." Beth stood. "Probably shouldn't have skipped lunch. Besides, I have another errand to run. I'll take the map and the book." She moved toward the front of the store.

Tom grabbed the book Beth wanted and met her at the counter. "Plan on doing some sightseeing?"

"Not exactly. Thought I might take some photographs, but I'm not sure what there is to see."

"You a photographer?" Tom entered the items into the register and hit the total button.

"I used to be — in my spare time."

"Well, this place is as good as any to indulge in one's hobby. That'll be eighteen seventy-three." He collected the woman's twenty and handed back her change.

"Do you have a hobby?" Beth asked. Tom was glad to see some color coming back into her face.

"Books..." He swept his hand in an arc. "...are my hobby — and wine." He bagged the map and book along with the receipt and slid them across the counter.

"Those are some hobbies I could probably get into." She smiled at Tom again. "Thanks for the help." As Beth turned toward the door, Annie got to her feet and shuffled toward her.

"Looks to me like that dog minds you pretty well," he said.

The woman let out a soft, easy laugh. "I suppose she does when she wants to." She held the door open until Annie passed through. "Bye now."

"Come back soon." Tom watched out the window until Beth was out of sight. Then he sat back down at the computer and continued perusing his email messages. If the poet didn't confirm soon, Tom would have to find someone to replace him.

CHAPTER 7

"**N**ot again! This piece of equipment is possessed!" Sandy slammed the door on the photo machine and stomped into the back room.

Amy Thompson gave her customer a nervous chuckle and shrugged her shoulders. "It appears my clerk is having technical difficulties." She finished the transaction and hurried toward the back as soon as the man left the store. "Sandy, what the heck is the matter?" she called as she approached the door and was practically knocked down when her hired help bolted, her ponytail whipping from side to side as she power-walked through the store.

"I am done! That machine has stressed my psyche, and I need a yoga session and some herbal tea."

"But you just came back from lunch!" Amy chased her to the front door. "When are you coming back?"

"If all goes well, I'll be fine in the morning," Sandy said over her shoulder without slowing down.

"Morning? But..." Amy stopped short when the front door slammed in her face. "Now my psyche is stressed." She sighed. "Might as well see what I can do with the evil photo machine." She had most of it disassembled when the bell on the front door jangled. "Be right with you," she called from where she knelt on the floor.

"Where are you?"

Amy peered around the Fuji 340 Minilab. "Hi, Beth.

48

Hang on a second." She made one final adjustment and clicked all the components back into place. Then she got to her feet and walked over to where Beth was waiting. "Don't tell me you're out of oil already?"

"Oil? Oh no, I..." Beth paused. "Well, you see, I've been taking some pictures of the area and bringing the rolls of film here to be developed."

"They turned out okay didn't they? We're breaking in a new machine and it hasn't been very cooperative."

"Oh yes, they were fine. In fact, well — I have something to show you." She held out the small bundle she'd been holding. "When I heard you discussing those photo cards with your clerk a while ago, I thought maybe I could take some pictures that you would like better." Beth unrolled the bundle, placed the photo cards she'd put together on the counter, and spread them out.

"These are wonderful," Amy said picking up each card and looking at it closely. "Much better than the ones I have for sale now."

"You really think so?"

"They're perfect. How many copies of each do you have?"

"Just these. I wasn't sure you'd like them."

"Like them? I love them. I'd take at least five copies of each one." Amy hesitated. "You know, some of the other merchants in town would probably like to see these too. Have you shown them to anybody else?"

"No. Do you really think they'd be interested?"

"Sure. And they'll love the fact that it's a local photographer making the cards. How much do you want for them?"

Beth's eyes widened. "I have no idea."

"Well, let's figure it out, shall we?" Amy grabbed a notebook and calculator from under the counter. Within a few minutes, she and Beth had worked out a wholesale and retail price that would give each of them a tiny profit per card. "How long do you think it'll take you to put together my order?"

"I need to have you print the photos, and I need to pick up more card making supplies first," Beth said, gathering up the cards.

"You might want to see who else would like these, that way I can print all the photos at once." Amy noticed some uncertainty in Beth's face. "Start small. I'm sure Tom over at the Headlands Bookstore would want some and maybe the place where you buy the card stock. Then come back with your negatives and we'll get this partnership going."

"Sounds like a good idea. Don't want to take on more than I can handle."

"Great. I'll check out the photo machine and make sure it's working properly. How about you drop by tomorrow morning, and I can have the pictures ready in a couple of hours." *That is if my clerk hangs around long enough.*

"That'll be fine. See you then." Beth opened the front door but didn't go out right away. "You really think they're good enough?" she asked turning back toward Amy.

"Positive. You'll see."

Beth smiled and nodded. Then she left the store, letting the door close behind her.

Tom Miller checked the recipe he'd clipped from the Sunday issue of the San Francisco Chronicle before dumping the large tiger shrimp into the stir-fry.

"Did Beth come in to see you today?" Amy asked, reclining against the counter.

Tom stopped chopping. "How did you know that?"

"Because I sent her. She came into the store today,

and when she told me she'd been taking pictures, I asked if she was happy with the prints that blasted machine had made. That damn thing seems to have a mind of its own."

"Hand me that sesame oil, please," Tom said pointing to the small bottle behind her.

Amy passed over the oil and then continued. "Anyway, she says she has something to show me and pulls out these photo cards. I thought they were great and suggested she ask the owners of some of the other shops to see if they would be interested in selling them as well."

"Oh, I see. I couldn't figure out why she came in with them out of the blue. They're actually very good photos. In fact, I asked her to come to the next reading, so folks could see her work."

"Really? What'd she say?"

"That she'd have to think about it. I really think I caught her off guard. I don't know what it is, but I get the feeling that she is not comfortable around people," he said, drizzling the oil over the shrimp and vegetables. Then he pulled the wok off the burner. "The stir-fry's ready. Grab a plate."

"Smells delicious." Amy piled her plate with shrimp.

"Here, try some of this chardonnay," Tom said, handing Amy a glass. "I brought it back from the Anderson Valley a couple of trips ago. I think you'll like it."

"Right again," she said after taking a sip. Then she carried her plate and glass of wine over to the black leather sofa.

"What are you doing?" Tom asked, standing next to the table and holding his own plate and glass of wine.

"Getting comfortable." She slipped off her shoes and curled her feet underneath her. After setting her wine glass on the black coffee table, she began devouring the food on her plate. "This is really good. You can make it any time, as long as you invite me."

"I'm surprised your taste buds come in contact with it long enough to tell how it tastes," Tom said under his breath as he crossed the large room to join her. He'd never seen anyone enjoy food as much as she did.

"What'd you say?" Amy asked around a mouthful of stir-fry.

"I'm glad your taste buds like it. And don't spill anything on my new furniture."

"Not to worry. I don't want to waste a single bite."

Taking Amy's advice, Beth Braddock had stopped by the other stores on the way home. Both Tom and the owner of the art supply shop wanted multiple copies of each one. Beth had been astounded. As she sat at the kitchen table figuring out how many reprints she would need of each picture, she began to realize how much work it was going to be. Not that she didn't have all the time in the world. "Hey, old girl," she said to Annie, who was lying at her feet. "Maybe I should call Tony and tell him all about my new business." Annie raised her head and gave Beth her best canine smile, her tail thumping approval.

"I'm really glad you called," Tony said a few minutes later. "Steve and I have been worried about you."

"I know you have, but I'm doing better."

"I can hear it in your voice. I'll be sure and tell Steve all about your new enterprise as soon as he gets home."

"When you do, be sure to mention that this whole thing came about because of you."

"How's that?"

"Well, if I didn't have to go get the oil, I never would've heard Amy talking about the photo cards. And if you hadn't saved my camera, I wouldn't have been able to take the pictures, so I guess that makes this whole thing your fault."

"Maybe it's just part of my evil plot to get your life back on track."

"Yeah, well maybe it's working."

Tony laughed. "Good. Craig would be proud of you. Talk to you later, Gorgeous."

Shameless flirt. Beth hung up and traded the phone for her cup of instant cappuccino sitting on the table next to her rocking chair. Sipping the warm drink as she rocked, she looked out over the bay.

Suddenly, a wave of loneliness swept over her, and she yearned to have Craig's arms around her. Without warning, tears filled her eyes. She swiped at them with the back of her hand as they rolled down her face.

Annie came out of the kitchen, where she had been having a snack, and put her head in Beth's lap. Beth reached down and scratched the dog's ears. "I don't know what I'd do without you, old girl," she said. "Maybe I should call Tony back and talk with him a while." Beth picked up the phone and dialed Tony's number but hung up after the second ring. *Hearing the emotion in my voice would just upset him.* Perhaps it was his voice, so much like Craig's, that started this whole thing anyway. No, what she needed was a good night's sleep.

She set her unfinished beverage in the sink and wandered into the bedroom. Annie, anticipating her next move, was already waiting on the bed. Beth changed into her nightgown and crawled between the cool sheets. Sleep was kind to her, enveloping her in its blackness soon after she laid her head on the pillow.

CHAPTER 8

The rose garden had always been Margaret's pride and joy. For almost forty years, she selected and nurtured over a hundred rose bushes of varying color, shape, and fragrance. Any weed that dared to poke its head through the topsoil was promptly plucked from existence. But that was before she got sick. As the strength waned from her frail body, Paul Hayden's mother was forced to abandon those things that brought her pleasure. By the time she escaped her earthly bonds, her garden was so overgrown it was impossible to tell the roses from the ragweed.

Working most of the afternoon, Paul nearly had one of the rose beds freed of its tangle of weeds when a Harley rumbled past. Standing to stretch his legs, he was surprised to see the motorcycle flip a U-turn and park in front of the bed & breakfast. Knowing Clara was most likely watching Judge Judy, he rinsed off his hands with the hose and dried them on his jeans as he headed toward the front door.

The rider was decked out in black leather and a matching full-face helmet with a polarized shield. Quite tall and rather lean, he returned Paul's wave and followed him into the small lobby.

"Looking for a place for the night?" Paul asked as he stepped behind the counter.

The man in black nodded.

"Well sir, I'll need you to fill this out." Paul laid a registration card on the counter.

Without a word, the rider pulled off his black gloves, revealing perfectly manicured hands with long nails painted bright red.

"Uhh..." Paul stammered.

A low, raspy laugh that somehow seemed familiar erupted from under the helmet as the rider pulled it off and shook out a head of platinum blond hair. "Oh Mr. Hayden, you should have seen the look on your face."

"Gladys! What the devil are you doing here?"

"I'm on my way to Portland."

"On a motorcycle?"

Gladys laughed again. "Guess there are a few things you don't know about me." She began filling out the registration card. "You see, my late husband, Carl, got me interested in bikes when we first starting dating. After he passed away ten years ago, I decided to keep riding." She pulled a thin wallet out of the inside pocket of her jacket, drew out a credit card, and slid it across the counter. "What do I owe you for one night?"

"I can't do that," Paul said, pushing it back toward her.

"You don't accept credit cards?" Gladys frowned.

"No. I can't charge you. You're practically family."

"That's very sweet of you, but I insist. Besides, I'll be expecting the full treatment."

Paul hesitated. He really felt awkward charging the woman who had been his assistant for almost two decades. "Fine, we'll do it your way, but it'll be at a discounted rate. A severely discounted rate."

"Deal. I'll get settled in, and then you can give me the grand tour."

While his new guest retrieved her bag from the Harley, Paul grabbed a set of fresh towels and a key to her room.

"Come down to the dining room when you're ready," he said as they climbed the stairs.

Deciding the gardening could wait for another day, Paul put away his tools and stopped by Clara's bungalow to let her know there'd be one more for dinner. Then he went into the dining room and fired up the espresso machine. He was sitting at his usual table, sipping an Americano when Gladys came in. She'd traded her leathers for magenta slacks and a light pink sweater.

"Oh, that coffee smells heavenly," she said joining him. "Is it from that espresso machine I found for you?"

He nodded. "Can I make you one?"

"How about a caramel latte?"

"Coming right up."

As Paul prepared Gladys' coffee, he heard Clara come in the back door and begin rattling pots and pans, a good indicator that the cooking was about to commence.

"So tell me, how long are you on vacation?" Paul asked as he set a heavy, oversized mug in front of Gladys. The milk had frothed nicely, creating a swirl of foamy peaks.

"This isn't exactly a vacation. It's more of a retirement."

"Retirement! But you're so young!"

"Thanks for the compliment, but I am sixty-seven years old. Besides, the man they hired to replace you was fresh out of college. I just didn't have the energy, or the inclination, to train another executive." She smiled at Paul. "No offense."

He laughed. "None taken. When you finish your drink, we should have just enough time for a tour before I must report for duty."

"I thought you were the boss."

"Not in the kitchen. In there, Clara rules supreme."

As if on cue, the short chef pushed through the door,

carrying the silverware tray and a stack of fresh napkins. She deposited her load on the closest table and headed back toward the kitchen.

"Clara," Paul called, "there's someone I'd like you to meet. Gladys, this is..."

"Clarabelle!"

His surrogate parent faltered mid-step and stared in disbelief. "Gladiola?"

Paul's gaze switched from one face to the other and back again. "You two know each other?"

"Know each other, we grew up together," Gladys said, getting to her feet and giving Clara a huge hug.

"Be a dear," Clara said to Paul, "and check on the roast. We have a lot of catching up to do." The two women sat down at Paul's table. "And bring me one of those new-fangled coffees."

After fixing another caramel latte, Paul went into the kitchen and began preparing dinner. Fortunately, the meat and potatoes were already in the oven, and the rolls were on a baking sheet waiting to go in next. He put the vegetables into the steamer and made the salad. By the time the other guests drifted in for dinner, Paul had the first course on the serving table and was slicing the roast.

"All right, let's get this food served," Clara said as she stumped into the kitchen. "Gladys and me are taking our supper to my place. I'll wash up the pots and pans, and you can do the rest."

"Yes ma'am," Paul said, wiping his sweaty brow on a corner of his apron. "Whatever you say."

After picking up the reprints and other supplies, Beth Braddock spent the next several days romping on the trail with Annie and assembling photo cards. She worked on

Amy's order first and took it to the gift shop as soon as it was done.

"I'm so glad you're here. I have everything ready." Amy had cleared the old photo cards out of the display and placed them in a wire basket where a sign declared them fifty percent off. "The tourists have started passing through, and I just know these will sell quickly," she said, placing Beth's cards on the rack.

"Do you really think so?"

"You bet. They love mementoes and these cards are terrific. Can I get your phone number? That way I can call you when I need more." Amy slid a notepad and pen toward Beth.

"Sure." Beth wrote down her name and number.

"Now that we've taken care of business, I'd like to take you for that latte I promised." Amy stepped out from behind the counter and walked toward the back of the store. "Sandy, hold down the fort. I'll be back in a little while."

Her clerk appeared in the doorway. "You got it, Boss Lady."

Amy let out a strange chuckle. "Come on," she said to Beth, "let's go."

"Where exactly are we going?" Beth asked as she hurried after Amy along Lansing Street.

"Just around the corner. A friend of mine has an espresso machine in his bed & breakfast."

Beth immediately recognized the place as one she'd photographed. Now she'd get to see what it looked like on the inside.

Amy trotted up the steps and pushed through the large, ornate front door. As Beth followed her inside, she felt as though she had traveled back in time. On the left-hand side of the foyer, a stairway led up to a landing, made a ninety-degree turn to the right, and continued up to the second story. Tucked underneath, a carved wooden counter served as the registration desk. An old-fashioned block of pigeonholes hung on the wall to the right, and a gigantic fern squatted in the other corner where the stairs were too low to walk under. Peering into the room on her right, she was drawn in by the intimate coziness of the overstuffed furniture huddled around the brick fireplace.

"Beth?" Amy called.

Startled, Beth hurried back to the small lobby.

Amy was there waiting for her. "Thought I'd lost you. Come on, Paul's making our lattes. I hope you like vanilla." She guided Beth into the dining room, where five antique tables of various sizes and shapes filled the room. Each had matching chairs, and the tops were polished to a high gloss. "Let's sit here." She pulled out a chair at the smallest table. "I'll introduce you as soon as he's done." She nodded toward the back of the room.

The man operating the espresso machine was at least six feet tall and wore his dark, wavy hair longer than most men. His tight jeans and black T-shirt accentuated his broad shoulders and narrow waist. "Here we are, ladies," he said, clutching two cappuccino mugs. He placed them on the table and, grabbing another chair and turning it around, straddled it as he joined them.

"Beth Braddock, Paul Hayden." Amy said, pulling her latte closer.

"Pleased to meet you." He offered his hand, and she shook it.

"Beth is our new resident photographer."

"Really? That's great."

"It's more of a hobby," Beth confessed. "You have a lovely place here," she said, hoping to guide the conversation away from herself.

"Thanks. I inherited it from my mother when she died a few months ago."

"Oh, I'm sorry to hear that."

"It's okay. She'd been sick for a long time and hadn't been able to do the things she enjoyed. In the end she was looking forward to being with my dad again. She never quite got over losing him."

Seconds ticked away until Beth realized she was staring at him. Embarrassed, she turned back to Amy. "So these are pretty good, huh?"

"Oh, by the way," Paul said, "I tried not to pile the foam so high this time." He winked at Amy as he crossed his arms on the back of the chair. She smiled, but Beth saw the color of her face darken slightly.

Beth took a sip. "Mmm, this is delicious."

"Told you they were the best." Amy smiled at Paul. "And Clara's coffeecake is scrumptious."

"How often do you come here?" Beth asked after taking another sip.

Amy looked at her over the rim of her cup.

"Almost every day," Paul chimed in. "And sometimes twice in one day."

"Really?"

Amy shrugged. "What can I say? I love lattes."

CHAPTER 9

"These are really very good," Tom Miller said as he arranged Beth's photo cards in the old map rack he'd found in the basement. "They'll easily sell." He stepped back and checked the rack's placement on the counter — conspicuous but not an obstruction.

"So," he turned to Beth, "have you made your decision?"

"I'm sorry, decision?"

"About coming to the next reading." He moved behind the counter and opened the cash register. "Nothing will get your new enterprise going like exposure." He chuckled as he paid Beth for the cards. "A little photography humor."

"Oh, yes." Beth smiled. "When is the next one?"

"Let me see." He leaned over and tapped a couple of keys on his computer. "Week from tomorrow. I'm sure Amy can get you a couple of enlargements printed by then." He closed the cash drawer and moved back around the counter.

Beth's smile vanished. "Enlargements?"

"Well, sure. Thought we'd put a couple of your favorite shots on display. Then sometime during the evening, I'll introduce you and point them out. You know, kind of like a commercial."

"A commercial, huh?" Beth frowned, apparently deep in thought. "I don't know."

"Well, think about it. Even if you decide you don't want to be introduced as a photographer, you should come for the reading. If for no other reason than to try the fantastic wine I found on my last trip."

"Sounds nice." Beth coaxed Annie from her place on the rug and started for the door. Turning, she said, "Well, I guess I could bring a couple of photos. What time on Thursday?"

"Around seven. Come a little earlier and we'll get your pictures set up."

"Okay. See you then." Beth and Annie left the store and headed down Main Street.

Tom brought up the flyer for the reading and updated it with Beth's name. He smiled as the printer spewed out its copies. An opportunity to share books and wine always put him in a good mood.

With negatives in hand and Annie in tow, Beth Braddock returned to the gift shop the next day and found Amy talking to the owner of the bed & breakfast.

"Good morning," Amy said. "I've got another customer for you."

"Oh?" Beth noticed how the man's dark eyebrows accentuated his jade-colored eyes.

"I was showing Paul your photo cards, and he'd like some to sell at the bed & breakfast."

"Well, I have one last order I'm working on now. Um...I can stop by with some samples in the next couple of days."

"I like what you brought Amy. Maybe just a couple of each shot. I don't get as much traffic at the bed & breakfast."

"Okay. I can probably get them done and to you in a week or two."

"That'll be fine." Paul smiled, showing his perfect white teeth. "I'll see you then, if not sooner," he said, strolling out the door.

Beth watched the man walk down the street until he was out of sight. When she turned back to speak to Amy, the woman was staring right through her. "He seems like a really nice guy." Beth offered a smile but didn't get one in return.

"Uh-huh."

"Have you known him long?"

"Uh-uh."

Uncomfortable with the conversation, she changed the subject. "I need to have a couple of eight-by-tens made. Can you print them? Tom seemed to think that you could."

Amy's face changed expression. "Tom?"

"Yes. He's invited me to the reading next week, and he wanted me to bring some enlargements. Wants to introduce me as a local photographer." Beth leaned in closer. "I'm a little nervous about it," she whispered.

"Oh don't be. It'll be great." The woman's smile returned. "Besides, what better way to show people your work."

"That's what he said."

After giving Amy her order, Beth left the gift shop and started toward Main Street. Annie, who had been exploring the nearby field, soon joined her. "Did you make a new friend?" Beth asked the old dog. "I think I did, and he has the greenest eyes I have ever seen."

* * *

Thursday arrived sooner than expected, and Beth spent most of the morning trying to decide what to wear.

Choosing a long floral skirt and a lightweight yellow sweater, she turned her attention to the five enlargements Amy had printed for her.

Looking them over, Beth was disappointed in most of them. The one looking at Mendocino from the headland was okay, but print of the sea lions lounging on the rocks wasn't good; they were too far away. The picture of the fishing boat had too much glare, and the shot down on the beach was too foggy. The photograph of the Mendocino Bed & Breakfast, however, was excellent. Its whitewashed driftwood sign and white picket fence were a good contrast to the green foliage and brought out the white blossoms on the huge tree in front. She hadn't selected it for a photo card because it looked cluttered, but she liked the detail in the larger print.

Beth left the house about twenty minutes after six with the two enlargements she liked and received an unhappy send off from Annie who, first of all did not like being left behind and second did not like being chained to the water tank. As Beth continued up the street, she wondered if Annie was trying to tell her something.

When she got to the bookstore, Tom was there to help her with the pictures. He put them next to her photo cards on a couple of wire racks that he used to display books. "Write your name and phone number on this." He pointed to a pen and a piece of paper on the counter between the photos. "That way people can contact you, or they can put their name and number, and you can get ahold of them." Just as she finished, Tom handed her a glass of wine. "Here. Now just relax and enjoy yourself."

"Thank you."

"It's one of my favorite merlots. Excuse me, duty calls." Tom left Beth standing in Annie's spot on the rug and greeted a couple as they walked through the door.

Looking around, Beth noticed that several folding chairs had been arranged facing the large, overstuffed chair that dominated the front corner of the bookstore. As more and more people entered the bookstore, her courage began to dwindle. The fact that most of them seemed to know each other didn't help. She was about to excuse herself when she recognized the man coming through the door. He was wearing brown Dockers and a plaid shirt, which he wore with the sleeves rolled up.

"Hi, Beth," he said when he spotted her.

"Hello, Paul. Have you come for the reading?"

"Yes and to see your prints."

Beth smiled. "They're over by the rack of photo cards," she said, pointing toward the counter. Paul excused himself and went over to look at them. Then he got himself a glass of wine and returned to where Beth was waiting.

"I really like the one of my bed & breakfast. Would you be willing to sell me a bigger enlargement? It would look great hanging in the lobby."

"Really? I guess so." Beth took a deep breath and relaxed her shoulders. She raised her glass to her lips and had another sip of wine. It tasted so good.

"Shall we find a place to sit?"

"Sure."

Paul led her over to a couple of chairs off to the side of the room. "Are these okay?" he asked.

Beth nodded. As she made herself comfortable, Amy arrived and took over pouring the wine. Freed from that responsibility, Tom made the rounds, greeting each new arrival personally. When everyone had something to drink, Amy came over.

"So glad to see both of you here. These are always so much fun."

"It's so generous of Tom to do this," Beth said.

"Oh, don't be fooled." Amy sat sideways in the chair in

front of them and leaned her arms across the back. "He puts out a collection jar to help pay the readers and writes off the wine as part of his promotional costs. He's quite the business man. Not to mention that he gets to spend the evening talking about his two favorite things, books and wine. So how are things at your place?" she asked Paul.

"Starting to pick up some. I think we're almost booked up for the weekend in fact."

"And how is Clara?"

"Bossy as ever. Oh say, that reminds me. She's making her famous cinnamon rolls tomorrow, so if you want to come by in the morning, I'll see that you get one."

"Sounds yummy. I'll be there bright and early." Amy glanced toward Tom. "Oops, gotta go. Looks like we're about to get started. Talk to you later." She hopped to her feet and headed back to the wine table.

"I think I'm going to get a refill," Paul said, holding up his empty glass. "Would you like some more?"

"No thanks, I'm fine."

Beth watched him talk and laugh with Amy as he got more wine. A few moments later, he was back and settled in next to her. Listening to the first author read his poetry, Beth continued to sip from her glass of wine and began to feel its warmth spread through her body. When the first reading was over, Tom moved to the podium.

"Thank you John, for sharing your wonderful poems with us. Before we have our next author read, I'd like to introduce Beth Braddock," Tom said, holding his hand out toward Beth. "She is a resident photographer who has agreed to share some of her photos with us tonight."

Looking around, Beth shifted in her chair; everyone was staring at her.

"I've put a sign-up sheet next to her photos in case anyone is interested in purchasing photos or cards from her, or you can talk with her after the reading. And now I'd like to introduce Claudia Bennett."

Beth had a hard time concentrating and suddenly felt very uncomfortable. She'd come to Mendocino in hopes of dissolving into the community but instead was the center of attention. The more she thought about meeting people the more nervous she got. Finally she couldn't stand it anymore. "I'm not feeling well," she whispered, leaning toward Paul, "I need to go home."

"Hang on a second, and I'll walk you." He took Beth's glass and stashed it under his chair along with his own, which was still half-full. "Come on." He took her arm and guided her to the door.

"You don't have to do this. I'll manage just fine."

"Not a problem. Besides, I could use some fresh air myself." He wrapped his left arm around her shoulders, pushed the door open with his other hand, and guided her outside.

All but just a glimmer of light had faded from the sky. Breathing in the crisp sea air, Beth started down the street. "I just live at the end of Main. You'll miss the second half of the reading."

"I don't mind, really. Are you feeling better?"

"Yes, a little." She paused. "Thanks."

They walked the next block in silence.

"How long have you been alone?" Paul asked, his face turned toward the ocean.

Beth stopped and stared at the man she barely knew. "How on earth do you know that?"

He chuckled. "There have been three lonely women in my life. My father died when I was young. Clara, my cook, also lost her husband as did my secretary, Gladys. You have that same wistful look in your eyes. I just put two and two together and made a guess."

Beth continued down the sidewalk. "Eight months," she said after they crossed the street.

"I'm sorry. Was he sick?"

Beth shook her head; she could feel the tears building behind her eyes. "An accident — my fault."

"Your fault? How's that?"

"I was driving — a tire blew — we crashed and Craig..." She shook her head again and began walking faster.

"Beth, wait." Paul hastened his pace, matching her stride. "I didn't mean to pry."

"No, of course not. I'm sorry." She stopped when she reached her gate. "Thanks for seeing me home." She held out her hand.

Paul took it in both of his. "My pleasure. Are you sure you'll be all right?"

Beth nodded as she pulled her hand away. Then she stepped through the gate and latched it behind her. She was halfway up the sidewalk when she realized she'd left without her photos.

As if reading her mind, Paul called, "I'll tell Tom you'll come by to pick up your prints." With one last wave, he headed back to the bookstore.

Amy Thompson looked toward the door again. Still no sign of them, and Claudia was almost finished. Where could they be?

"How are we doing on the wine?" Tom asked, joining her at the table.

"What? Oh, fine. There's at least two bottles of each left."

Tom scanned the crowd. "Where's Beth?"

"She and Paul left just after Claudia started."

"Left? Well, what about the people who want to talk to her about her pictures?"

Amy shrugged. She was about to say something when Paul walked through the door, alone. He quietly returned to his seat, retrieved his wine glass, and finished off its contents. Amy was practically dancing in place by the time the reading was over. As soon as the applause started, she scooted across the room. "Where did you run off to, and where's Beth?"

"She said she wasn't feeling well, so I walked her home."

"Is she all right?" Amy studied Paul's face.

He smiled. "She'll be just fine. The wine must have gone to her head." He winked and strolled over to where Tom stood next to Beth's photos.

There was something about the way he looked when he talked about Beth. Amy couldn't say for sure, but there was something.

CHAPTER 10

Tom Miller looked at his reflection in the bathroom mirror. How many glasses of wine did he have anyway? Amy said something about two bottles of each left, but all he remembered putting away were two bottles of sauvignon blanc and one pinot noir. That left five bottles unaccounted for. A few regulars had stayed to talk rather than drink wine. Of course, Amy had stayed, Paul too, and they had more wine while putting the bookstore back in order.

"Probably just coming down with something," he muttered to himself as he popped three ibuprofen in his mouth and washed them down with a big gulp of coffee. He felt better after his shower and decided to take Paul up on his offer of fresh cinnamon rolls but would probably pass on the latte. No sissy drinks for him.

As he trudged down the stairs, he toyed with the idea of driving over but decided the walk would help clear his head. Grateful he'd worn his brown leather jacket, he hustled through the fog-chilled air toward the bed & breakfast.

A warm, cinnamonny smell greeted Tom as he strode up the sidewalk. It intensified and enveloped him as he stepped inside. Following the sound of clinking utensils, he spied Amy sitting at a small table in the far corner.

"Good morning," Tom said, joining her.

"Morning. How's your head?" Amy grinned at him.

"What do you mean?" He took off his jacket and hung it on the back of his chair.

"I thought it might feel a little foggy, considering how much wine you had last night."

"Oh, come on." Tom pushed the sleeves of his cashmere sweater to his elbows. "I had no more wine that anyone else."

Paul entered the small dining room, carrying two carafes of coffee.

"Hey, Tom, glad you decided to come. Coffee?" he asked when he reached their table.

"Please." Tom turned over the cup sitting in front of him.

"Leaded or unleaded?" Paul said, raising each carafe in turn.

"By all means, leaded."

Paul filled his cup with the steaming, brown liquid. "So how's the head this morning?"

Tom's eyes shifted from one face to the other. "What's with you two? I didn't have that much to drink." He paused. "Did I?"

"Well..." Paul winked at Amy and headed back toward the kitchen, refilling cups as he went.

Tom picked up his cup and blew across the top of it. Ignoring the warning from the voice in his head, he took a small sip, which instantly burned his top lip and the tip of his tongue. Deciding to let it cool, he set the cup of coffee down on the table. "So, where are those cinnamon rolls that are supposed to be so wonderful?"

"Coming right up," Amy said, nodding toward the kitchen door.

Before Tom had a chance to turn around, Paul deposited two plates on the table. The breakfast pastry was at least four inches across and almost as tall. It was the most gigantic cinnamon roll Tom had ever seen.

Paul laughed. "I wish you could see the look on your face. Your eyes are just about the size of these rolls. Don't be shy. Dig in before they get cold." He sat down in the extra chair at their table.

Tom tore off a piece; it oozed icing and spices. Slowly he placed it in his mouth.

"Oh my," Amy said around her own mouthful. "You're so right Paul. These are even better than the coffeecake. I didn't think it possible but..." She shoved another piece into her mouth. "Mmmmmm."

Beth Braddock finished her walk on the headland trail and continued up Ukiah Street to the small market a few blocks from her house. She found a nice assortment of summer squash and her favorite variety of tomatoes. There were strawberries big enough to fill a teacup and fragrant melons. As she came outside to retrieve Annie, Beth noticed a man walking toward her, wearing faded denim jeans and a white T-shirt. As he got closer, she realized it was Paul.

"Good morning Beth," he said when he got close enough. "How are you today?"

"Oh, much better. Thank you."

The chocolate lab sat down between them, her mouth agape and her tongue lolling. "And who is this?" He bent down and rubbed the dog's ears.

"This is Annie."

"Well, hello Annie. You look like a happy dog."

"Spoiled would be a more accurate description."

Paul straightened. "Did you get your prints back?"

"No, not yet."

"You know, Tom said something about keeping them there, if you want." He laughed. "Of course, he may not remember."

"Why is that?"

"Too much wine. You still willing to sell me that enlargement of the bed & breakfast? I'm sure Suzy over at the art gallery knows someone who can mat it for me."

"Sure. I'll check with Amy to see how long it will take to get one printed. How big did you want it?" Beth shifted the bags of groceries from one hand to the other.

"Oh, an eleven-by-fourteen should be about right. Not too big, the lobby is kind of small."

"Okay. I'll let you know when I bring your cards by."

"Sounds good. If you come by in the afternoon, we can talk about the picture while we get a bite to eat."

"You mean go out?"

"Not officially, just two friends having dinner. Besides it'll give me an excuse to sneak away for the evening. And if we go around five o'clock, the Bay View Café has great seafood entrees on the early bird special."

"Okay, I'll call you when I get the cards done. Come on, Annie. Let's go." The dog looked up at Paul one last time, got to her feet and fell in behind her master.

Beth thought about Paul as she strolled home. When she opened the gate, she realized she'd been humming.

An hour later, several stacks of photo cards covered the table. "I need a break," she told Annie as she stood and stretched, trying to loosen her stiff back. "Guess this would be a good time to check on my pictures." A few minutes later, she pushed through the door of the bookstore.

Tom was talking with an elderly gentleman at the far end of the counter. The man's jaunty hat reminded Beth of her grandfather. "Be with you in just a moment," Tom called, barely glancing her way. Beth flipped through a book of poetry while she waited for him to finish up with his customer and slide down the counter to where she was waiting.

"So how are you? Feeling better, I hope."

"Yes thank you," Beth replied. "I thought I'd pick up my pictures."

"Like I was telling Paul, you're welcome to leave them here, if you like. Seems several people are interested in them. Your cards, too." He pulled a large envelope out from under the counter. "Their names and phone numbers are written down on a piece of paper, as well as a couple of shop owners who'd like some photo cards to sell. If anyone else is interested, I'll let you know."

"Gee, thanks," Beth said, taking the envelope.

"No problem. Feel free to bring some more to the next reading."

"I just might do that," Beth said as she walked out the door.

Since she was halfway there, Beth decided to talk to Amy at the gift shop about getting the enlargement made.

"One that size has to be special ordered. It'll probably take a couple of weeks," Amy said after Beth explained what she needed. "By the way, have you ever considered having your photos mounted to show at the gallery? Suzy is always looking for work to display."

"But this is just something to keep me busy," Beth confessed.

"Well, you should think about it. You have some really terrific photos."

As Beth returned home, she actually toyed with the idea, but only for about two seconds. *If I couldn't handle being at the bookstore, what would I do at the art gallery? Totally freak?*

She tossed the envelope on the kitchen table, fixed

herself a late lunch, and headed out on the trail with Annie. As the light faded, she watched the fog bank roll into shore, bringing with it the salty smell of the sea. The faraway sound of a buoy made her feel lonely but not necessarily alone. Not anymore.

CHAPTER 11

Paul Hayden leaned back in his swivel chair, stretching his arms over his head. He'd spent most of the morning paying bills and getting a deposit ready. A full house over the weekend had been exhausting but profitable. Business was picking up; tourist season had begun. With nothing reserved until Wednesday, there would be plenty of time to clean the rooms and get caught up on the laundry.

After turning off the small desk lamp, he stepped around the counter and opened the front door but halted when the phone rang. Leaning across the counter, he grabbed the portable phone off its charger. "Mendocino Bed & Breakfast."

"Uh, hello Paul? It's Beth."

"Oh, hi. Hey, does this mean my cards are done?"

"Yes, I just finished. When would you like me to bring them by?"

"Actually, I'm kind of busy right now. Why don't you bring them by around four-thirty? Then we can walk over to the café and have dinner."

"Are you sure? I don't want to impose."

"Nonsense. Don't have any guests and don't expect any, so Clara's taken the day off. If we don't go to dinner, I'll be stuck eating a tuna sandwich."

"Well, I guess we can't have that. What time did you say?"

"Four-thirty. See you then." Paul hung up and start-ed out the front door again. Hoping the day would pass quickly, he dove into his chores, whistling as he cleaned.

With the exception of the reading, Beth Braddock hadn't concerned herself about what clothes to wear. Jeans and a T-shirt were her usual attire. "I don't know what the big deal is," she told Annie, who'd followed Beth into the bedroom and made herself comfortable on the bed. "Like Paul said, it's just dinner with a friend, not a date for heaven's sake."

Nevertheless, she spent the rest of the afternoon try-ing on outfits until the closet was empty and the bedroom covered with discarded garments. Annie, bored with this strange activity, had gone to sleep. Finally, Beth decided on a sleeveless summer dress. The pale green color looked good against her skin, and she liked the way it flowed over her waist and hips. A light sweater and a pair of sandals added the final touches.

"Well, Annie, what do you think?" The old dog raised her head, opened her mouth and began panting. "Are you smiling approval or laughing at me?" Beth asked her.

Stepping into the bathroom, she wondered what to do about her hair. Her usual ponytail was too casual, but she didn't like the way her hair looked down. Pulling it up at the sides made her look younger and kept it out of her face. Pleased with how she looked, Beth coaxed An-nie outside and hooked up her chain. Then she headed up Albion Street.

With each step, she felt her heart beating faster. "Get a grip," she told herself, "it's just dinner. Besides," the voice continued, "he seems like an interesting person. Relax and have a good time."

When Beth entered the bed & breakfast, Paul was occupied with something behind the check-in counter. He smiled when he realized she was there. "Wow! You look terrific."

"Thanks." Beth reached up to smooth her hair. She could feel her face turning red. *Blushing?* She could hardly believe it and hoped Paul hadn't noticed. "Here are your cards." She handed him the small bundle she had tucked in the crook of her arm.

"Great." Paul stashed them under the counter. "Shall we go?" he asked, holding the door open for her. Turning left at the corner, they headed toward Main Street and the Bay View Café.

Seated at a table out on the little deck, they studied the menu, informed the waiter of their decisions, and Paul ordered a bottle of white wine. An uncomfortable silence fell over them until he finally asked, "So, when should my print be ready?"

"Oh, Amy said it should be here in about a week," Beth replied, relieved to have something to talk about. Then she picked up her water glass and took a sip.

"Good, I'm anxious to get it framed. I think it'll look great in the lobby. What other pictures have you taken that I haven't seen yet?"

Beth shook her head. "None. There's so many tourists right now, it's hard to get a shot without getting at least one of them in the picture."

Paul chuckled. "One of the hazards of living in a vacationers' hotspot." By the time their salads had arrived, their discussion had picked up momentum and moved on to other things.

"I have read more in the last year than I have in a long time," Beth said, pushing her salad around with a fork.

"I always seemed too busy before and now it helps me — well, escape."

"I like to read too, but I really enjoy writing," Paul said. "Something I never had time for when I was working."

"I used to write, too." The box of manuscripts tucked away in the front closet popped into her mind.

"Growing up I spent most of my time scribbling in a notebook, usually when I should've been doing my chores." Buttering a piece of bread, Paul smiled. "But after college, my job in Walnut Creek took up all my time. You see, I needed the money to help my mom with the bed & breakfast. But now that I've moved back to Mendocino, I find myself at my desk more often — usually writing sonnets," he confessed. "What kinds of things do you like to write?"

"Oh, I haven't written in a very long time. I used to write children's stories and occasionally a poem or two. I even started a novel but never finished it." Uncertain what to say next, she was relieved when she spotted the waiter approaching with their meal.

"For the lady, grilled halibut and shrimp scampi for the gentleman," the waiter said, placing the steaming plates on the table. "Anything else?"

"Beth?" Paul asked. She shook her head. "I think we're set for now," he told the waiter.

The conversation died momentarily as they savored the first few bites of their food. After sampling her fish, baked potato, and braised carrots Beth attempted to change the subject. "Where did you grow up?"

"Right here in Mendocino. My parents inherited the inn from my great-aunt, Lucile. But when we lost my dad in Vietnam, things got pretty tough for me and my mom. As soon as I was old enough, I'd do odd jobs to help bring in money." Paul picked up his wine glass like he was offering a toast. "And now I get to slow down and enjoy life."

"It must be a pleasant change for you."

"Sure is. What better place than Mendocino to sit at your window and write. Don't you agree?"

"Oh, I don't think I could. It's been too long."

"Well, if you change your mind, I'm thinking of taking a writing course this fall at the college in Fort Bragg. It might give you a way to get back into it. We could even ride together."

"It's very nice for you to offer, but..." Beth took another bite of halibut and then put her fork down.

"Something wrong?" Paul asked, refilling their wine glasses.

"Oh, no. I'm just really full. I haven't eaten this much in a long time. Guess my stomach isn't used to it." Beth smiled.

The waiter reappeared, as if on cue. "Can I interest you in dessert? Our special tonight is caramel latte cheesecake. Coffee flavored cheesecake drizzled with caramel and topped with shavings of dark chocolate."

"Ooh, that sounds good, but I don't know where I'd put it," Beth said.

"It does sound good. Why don't you bring us one with two forks." Paul winked at Beth. "That way we both can be miserable."

"Very good." The waiter picked up the plates and retreated to the kitchen.

After dinner, Paul walked Beth home where they were greeted with joyous barking and jumping. "She certainly is friendly."

"Demanding too. Thinks she's the queen of the house." Beth stopped outside the front gate and turned to Paul.

"Thanks for dinner. I had a great time," she said, extending her hand.

"So did I." This time Paul took her hand in his and kissed the back of it. "We'll have to do it again sometime."

"I'd like that." Beth stepped through the gate and latched it behind her. "Goodnight."

She watched Paul head back the way they had come. "Well, Annie," Beth said as she unhooked the dog's chain, "I don't know about you, but I had a wonderful evening."

CHAPTER 12

Amy Thompson stood, rubbed her back, and looked around. Sandy was nowhere in sight. "That girl does the best vanishing act when I need help," she murmured. Restocking was a chore Amy would rather delegate than do herself. She picked up the empty box and took it into the backroom.

"Hello?"

Amy knew immediately who it was.

"Mail call."

"Hi Jane," she said, as she moved toward the front of the store.

"Nothing interesting today," the mail carrier said, tossing a pile of envelopes on the counter.

"Thanks." Amy couldn't help but chuckle at Jane's nosy nature. Perhaps that was a prerequisite for working at the post office.

Flipping through the stack of mail, she came across her invitation to Art in the Gardens and smiled. When she first moved to Mendocino, she'd involved herself in every possible event, either volunteering or attending. Helping at the Botanical Gardens had been fun, but it had been hard work too. For the last three years, she only attended the event. "This would be a perfect opportunity to do something fun with Beth," she said out loud.

"What's that?" Sandy asked as she came in the front door.

"What?"

"Were you talking to me?"

"No, just thinking out loud." Amy shoved the invitation under the counter with the other mail. "Where were you?"

"Oh, I ran over to the market. I was dying for a mango," she said, holding up a small paper bag.

"Next time please let me know before you leave the store."

"You got it, Boss Lady." Sandy walked into the backroom and put the bag on the counter next to the tiny sink. She pulled out a knife and began cutting up the fruit.

The day had finally arrived. Tom Miller charged down the stairs, rounded the corner, and headed up Main Street, his anticipation building with each step.

Entering the bed & breakfast, he followed the familiar clink of utensils to the small table he'd begun to consider as his own. It wasn't until after he'd waved at Paul that he realized the bitter truth; he'd become a breakfast pastry junkie.

Bakery donuts and bear claws had never really done it for him. He could take them or leave them, usually the latter, but Clara's cinnamon rolls, coffeecakes, and even her muffins were in a class all by themselves. And today, Tom was to experience yet another of her creations — scones. Not just any scone, but a maple nut scone. Of all possible flavors, maple nut was his favorite.

Paul approached, coffee pot in one hand and a cluster of cups in the other. "Morning Tom," he said, setting one of them down and filling it.

"Morning." Trying to act casually, Tom continued. "Amy not here yet?"

"Don't think she's coming. Isn't she taking Beth to Art in the Garden today?"

"Oh yeah, that's right." Tom slowly took a sip of his coffee. "So, how'd those scones turn out?" he asked, trying his best to be nonchalant.

"I think they're the best I've ever tasted. Let me get rid of this stuff, and I'll join you." Paul moved back toward the kitchen, giving refills as he went. A few moments later, he returned with two plates and a cup of coffee for himself.

Tom revered the large, triangular pastry which lay before him. Coated with a shiny glaze, it was a thing of beauty to behold. He picked it up and gently broke it in two. The nutty aroma caressed his nose as he bit into one of the halves. Moister than any scone he'd ever had, he closed his eyes and savored its flavor like he did a fine wine.

"Aren't these delicious? Too bad Clara only makes these once a year."

Opening his eyes, Tom was surprised to see Paul had already consumed most of his own scone. He stopped mid-chew; surely he'd heard wrong. "Once a year?" he asked around the mouthful of scone.

Paul nodded. "For my birthday, which actually isn't until Thursday, but she only bakes on the weekends." He laughed. "I'm not sure how long they'll last." He leaned closer. "This is my third one today, but don't tell Clara."

Tom finished half of his scone before he spoke again. "Seems a shame to have to wait a year before enjoying another one of these. Can you freeze them?"

"I suppose so, why?"

"I'll explain in a minute. First let's talk about your birthday."

* * *

As Tom walked back toward his bookstore, a large take-out container in his hands, he pondered how to go about inviting Amy to an evening out. Finally he decided the less said, the better. *It will definitely be more fun that way.*

Amy Thompson parked her bright yellow, late model VW Bug in front of Beth's house and spotted her hooking Annie to the water tank with a long chain. The dog lay down and put her head on her paws. "Annie doesn't seem too happy," Amy said after getting out of the car.

"She's not." Beth looked back at the chocolate lab. "But I don't want her jumping out of the yard while I'm gone. I'll grab my purse and we can go."

Amy got back in her car and started it up.

"Boy, this sure is a lot quieter than my old Beetle used to be," Beth said as she settled into the front seat.

"You used to drive a Bug?" Amy pulled away from the curb, flipped a U-turn, and headed up Main Street toward Highway 1.

"Yes. It was one of my more foolish purchases."

"I got this when I traded in my BMW." Pausing only briefly enough to check both ways for oncoming traffic, Amy gunned the engine of the small car, hitting third gear before finishing the wide, sweeping turn and heading north.

"Why would you trade a BMW for a VW Bug?"

"Personally, I never did like that car, but my ex-husband just had to have it. It was all about image." Amy grimaced at the thought of Rick. He wasn't such a bad guy, just a lousy husband.

"Oh. My Bug had a rollback sunroof and had been chopped Baja-style." Beth smiled. "My husband, Craig, loved to drive that car."

"Men!" Amy shook her head.

"And he took great pleasure in doing donuts in the snow and scaring me to death," Beth added. "We went everywhere in that car, until I broke the crankshaft."

"How did you do that?"

"It died one day, and since I was going downhill, I popped the clutch. The crankshaft snapped right in half."

"Oh no!"

"I had to ride my ten-speed until we could afford another car."

"And I bet it wasn't a VW Beetle."

Beth smiled and shook her head. "Absolutely not."

They rode the rest of the way in silence until Amy maneuvered into the gravel parking lot of the Botanical Gardens and squeezed between two other vehicles. "I think you're going to like this," she said as they started toward the front gate. "I know it doesn't look like much from here but wait until we get inside." She linked arms with Beth. "Come on. I'll introduce you to Grace. She and her husband manage the place."

Amy led her through the entrance. "Hi, Rachel," she said, sliding two tickets across the counter.

"Hey, Amy."

"Where's Grace?"

"She's out in the information tent."

"Thanks." Amy smiled at Beth. "Follow me and try not to get lost."

Beth Braddock had never seen so many people occupying one place at one time, especially a place as beautiful as the gardens. Gravel pathways criss-crossed through miniature hills of green. The sun had finally broken through the high clouds, and small droplets of water sparkled in the sunlight. The fragrant white, pink, and purple blossoms of sweet peas clung to the fences. Tiny hedges of babies'-breath lined the lawn areas, and giant mounds of day lilies waved their flags of yellow and orange. Blue spears of lupine bravely stood guard against the crowd and cactus dahlias looked like pink sea anemones.

People meandered in all directions, and occasionally a person in a bright yellow vest hustled by, speaking into a hand radio. Beth could hear music coming from somewhere, but it was hard to tell what it was over the drone coming from the mass of people around her.

"This is the largest crowd I've seen," Amy said, stopping just inside the main gate. "The first year I moved here I was a volunteer. Those are the people wearing the vests," she said, pointing to a small group of them standing off to the side. "I never worked so hard in my life, but it was worth it. Come on, Grace is over this way."

They entered a huge white tent, where an older woman with curly grey hair sat behind a large table. "Amy! I'm so glad you're here," she said, getting to her feet and coming around the table.

"I wouldn't miss it for anything. Looks like you have a record crowd this year." Amy gave the woman a hug.

"We had so many artists respond and want space that we had to expand the display area into Meadow Lawn."

"Wow, I can hardly wait to see what you've done. Grace, this is Beth Braddock. She's a friend of mine from Mendocino."

"Hello." Grace extended her hand. "I'm so glad you're here."

"It's nice to meet you," Beth said, returning the handshake.

"Here's your map," Grace said, picking up a folded piece of paper. "And I reserved a picnic basket for you." She stepped back behind the table and placed a brightly colored basket in front of Amy. Beth could see small, clear containers filled with all kinds of unusual-looking foods.

"Thanks. I'll be sure and stop by on my way out."

"Be sure that you do." Grace winked at her. "Enjoy!"

Amy walked out of the tent and held the basket out to Beth. "Hold this a second while I scope out our first stop." Beth took the basket and looked around, trying to make sense of the scene before her. "Perfect," Amy said folding the map. "Let's head back up the path. Just around the corner is the glass blower who has a studio in Mendocino. He creates the most beautiful vases. Then we'll pick up a couple of wine glasses."

"Wine glasses?" Beth asked, shifting the basket.

"For the wine tasting. There are about ten wineries that come here every year. They may not be on Tom's list of top ten, but I think they have some good wine." Amy smiled as she took the basket out of Beth's hands and headed into the crowd. Beth hurried after her, not wanting to get separated.

Several feet up the trail, they stopped by a table covered with hand-blown vases. "Aren't they beautiful?" Amy asked.

"They're so delicate. I'd be afraid to use them," Beth said, picking up one to admire.

"Come on. Let's get our glasses. I'm dying to have some wine."

Beth gently set the vase back on the table and followed Amy to a pyramid of wine glasses on a small table. "Two, please," Amy said, setting the basket at her feet and tucking the map inside. The man behind the table plucked two glasses off the top and handed them to her. "Here you go," she said, passing one to Beth and picking up the basket again. Stepping over to the nearest wine tasting station, she balanced the basket on one hip and eagerly held out her glass. "How about some Chardonnay?" she said to the steward, and he filled her glass with a golden liquid.

"And for you?" he asked Beth.

"Anything dark red will be fine," Beth said, holding out her own glass.

The steward selected a tall, pale green bottle. "This is a syrah. Sweet vanilla frames the black currant and berry flavors, while dark chocolate adds to the complexity of the wine," he said as he filled Beth's glass.

Amy giggled. "Sounds like Tom," she whispered.

Laughing and talking as they sipped their wine, the pair wandered to the next wine tasting station. As the steward filled their glasses, the music started up again. This time it was coming from behind a large clump of rhododendron bushes. "Isn't that Celtic music?" Beth asked.

"I love Celtic music," Amy and Beth said in unison. Then they both laughed.

"Well, looks like we have something in common." Amy clinked her glass against Beth's. "Let's go check it out."

After listening to "Bedlam Boys" and "Follow Me Up to Carlow," Amy continued the tour of the gardens. Beth marveled at the huge variety of artwork on display, from jewelry to furniture. There were sculptures of all kinds and paintings done in oil or watercolor. Sand paintings, pottery, and decorated glassware covered tables set up in every nook and cranny of the gardens. Having followed pathways that turned right and left, often crossing each other, Beth didn't know where she was, but she didn't care. She was enjoying herself.

As Amy led her around yet another unexplored corner, she spied an enormous iris bed. "This must be something to see in the spring," Beth said, pointing at the tall spears of green. "I've never seen so many iris packed into one area."

"It really is spectacular. I think Grace has over one hundred varieties in there."

"Iris are my favorite flower. I used to have a rather large bed of them myself."

"We'll just have to come back next spring. The magnolias and camellias bloom then too."

"I'd like that," Beth said.

Amy checked the map again. "Let's head out toward Meadow Lawn. My favorite winery is there, and you've got to see the miniature forest that Geowonders brings. They specialize in bonsai, and it makes you feel like the jolly green giant."

"Lead on!" Beth said, waving her wine glass in front of her.

About one o'clock, Amy Thompson began to feel tipsy. "What do you say we take a break and have some lunch?" she asked Beth.

"I'd like that. I'm starving."

Amy led the way back toward the display house and sat down at a table in the middle of the rose garden. "This is one of my favorite spots," she said, as she began pulling things out of the basket. Reaching into her bag, she brought out two small plates and a sandwich bag with plastic utensils. "These small baskets are set up for one and I didn't think you'd want to eat off the same fork."

Beth laughed. "Good assumption. This all looks so good."

"Nothing but the best gets by Grace. Here try some of this herb cream cheese on your bread. It's her secret recipe." Amy divided the salad, fruits, and veggies between the two plates. Then she placed the box of Mendocino chocolates between them. "Race you to dessert."

"Thanks so much for taking me today," Beth Braddock said to Amy as the yellow VW sped across Russian Gulch. "I haven't enjoyed myself like that for such a long time."

"Thanks for going with me. It's more fun when you go with someone. I talked Tom into going one year, but he refuses to go back. Something about hanging out with amateurs, like he's some kind of expert. I think he just doesn't like the competition."

"I'd like to go back with my camera and get some shots of the foliage. I've never seen so many beautiful flowers in one place."

"That would be fantastic! I've been looking for pictures of flowers for my sun room but haven't found anything I like."

"Better wait to see..."

"What the —" Amy said as she pulled up in front of Beth's house for the second time that day.

Following her gaze, Beth was surprised to find Paul and Annie sitting on the front porch.

"Looks like you've got company." Amy turned off the engine and coasted to a stop. "So it would seem." Beth climbed out of the car and started up the front walk. "And what might the two of you be up to?" she asked the duo.

"Well, I realized I hadn't paid you for the first order and..."

"Oh my gosh, you're right. I'd forgotten all about it."

"So, when I came by and you weren't home yet, I decided to let old Annie here loose and play a little fetch with her. I figured she'd gotten bored waiting for you to get back."

"I see." Beth turned back to Amy, who was still sitting in the car. "Do you want to come in?"

"No thanks," she called through the open window. "I need to get home. Talk to you later." Then she started her car and sped off.

"How about you? Would you like to come in?" Beth asked Paul, as she started up the steps with Annie at her heels.

"Actually, I have to get back. I just wanted to give you this," he said, handing her a small white envelope, "and invite you to my birthday celebration." He followed her inside and made himself comfortable in the rocking chair. "Tom and I were talking this morning and decided to go somewhere special. It should an evening of good food and even better company."

"I'd love to," said Beth, tossing her jacket on the kitchen table. "When is this bash going to take place?"

"This coming Thursday. And unless you want to squeeze into the back of Amy's Bug or run alongside Tom's Z3, I'll take all of us in my rig."

Beth laughed. "Sounds great. What time will you be collecting everybody?"

"Oh, around six." Paul got up and walked toward the door.

"Thanks again for checking on her highness," Beth said, scratching the old dog's head. Annie's gaze shifted from Beth to Paul.

"My pleasure." He opened the door and stepped out onto the porch. "See you Thursday, if not sooner."

"It's a date," Beth said, following him outside.
Paul leapt down the steps and spun around, a large smile on his face. "Remember, you said it, not me." Before she could reply, he turned and, in three long strides, was out the gate and headed up Main Street.

CHAPTER 13

T he sun peeked through the scattered clouds and the faint breeze brought with it the pungent smell of the ocean. In the distance, Beth Braddock could hear the raucous bark of the sea lions as they reclined on their favorite rock.

She and Annie were halfway up the front walk when she heard the phone. Scrambling up the steps and bursting through the door, she managed to answer it before it stopped ringing.

"Beth?"

"Yes," she gasped, trying to catch her breath.

"It's Amy. Your enlargement is finally here, and it's fantastic. They did a really good job."

"Great. I'll be there in a few minutes to pick it up. Thanks for calling." Beth hung up and grabbed her wallet. "Come on old girl," she said to Annie. "Let's go pick up Paul's photo."

As she strolled up Main Street with her canine companion trotting beside her, she marveled at the scenery. It was one of those rare, bright, sunshiny days on the coast. Everything sparkled in the sunlight, and she felt like dancing her way to the gift shop. Leaving the dog at the door, she went inside.

"Boy, that was quick," Amy said coming from the back of the store. "Wait until you see this picture." She pulled a huge white envelope out from under the counter and removed the photograph. "What do you think?" she asked, handing it over.

Beth held it up at arm's length. The image was sharp, the color vivid. "It's perfect. I think Paul will be pleased." She felt a surge of pride as she slid it back into the envelope.

"Speaking of Paul, do you know where we're going tonight for his birthday?"

"Why no, I don't. He just said he'd come by to pick me up at six. Tom didn't tell you either?"

"Not a thing. Probably afraid I'd over plan the evening. Sometimes he can be so frustrating; I don't know why I put up with that man."

"I think he is rather charming."

"Then you can have him," Amy said, waving her hand.

"Oh, I didn't mean it that way." Beth hesitated, not sure what to say next. "I mean..."

"Just kidding, don't worry about it. But when you get to the bed & breakfast, see if you can get any information out of Paul."

"I'll see what I can find out." Beth started for the door. "Shall I..."

"Call me if he tells you anything," Amy broke in, following along behind her.

"Will do. Bye." Beth collected Annie, and as the pair started down Lansing Street, she began to hum, a feeling of happiness overwhelming her.

The bed & breakfast was strangely quiet when Beth stepped inside. "Hello?" she called as she moved toward the dining room. "Anyone here?"

"Be right out." The voice was definitely that of an older woman, so Beth assumed it was Clara. While she waited, she removed the photograph from its envelope and held it up to admire one more time.

Paul had mentioned hanging it in the lobby, but as Beth looked around the tiny foyer, she wondered where he would put it. The only wall space was behind the counter under the staircase. Wanting to see how it looked, she glanced back toward the dining room and then slipped behind the counter. With the envelope behind it like a mat, Beth held the picture against the vintage wallpaper. Paul was right; it looked perfect there.

"Is there something I can help you with?" Clara demanded.

Beth jumped so much she almost dropped the photo. "Oh, you startled me," she said, turning around to find the small cook standing on the other side of the counter with her hands on her hips. "I have Paul's photograph he ordered, and I was just seeing how it would look." She tried to slip it back into the envelope, but her hands were shaking so badly she couldn't do it.

"Here, let me have that." Clara took both items from Beth and laid them on the counter. "Didn't mean to scare you none. I've got the kettle on and was just about to have myself a cup of tea. Looks like you could use one to calm your nerves." She ushered Beth back around the counter and toward the dining room.

"I don't want to impose."

"Nonsense. If I didn't want the company, I wouldn't have asked you. Besides, Paul won't be back for quite a while. I sent him to Fort Bragg with a grocery list as long as his arm. Now, how do you take your tea?"

"Okay, I give. Where are we going?" Amy Thompson asked when Paul's two-tone grey Honda Element passed through Fort Bragg and continued up the Pacific Coast Highway. Certain they were heading for a place on the wharf, she had been surprised when they passed the turn off.

"You'll see," was the only reply she got from the two men in the front seat.

"Maybe this cloak and dagger stuff is kind of fun after all," she whispered to Beth. "But I can't let them know it." She leaned forward. "Oh come on, just one hint," she pleaded.

"Just sit back and enjoy the ride," Tom said without turning around.

"Sorry I didn't get any information," Beth whispered, "but Paul wasn't there when I stopped by."

"Don't worry about it. We'll find out soon enough." Amy settled back into her seat. "So how is the card-making business?"

"Not bad. I was just telling Tony the other night..."

"Your brother-in-law?"

"That's right. I was telling him that several places in town were willing to sell them, and every spare moment has been spent putting them together. In fact, I need some more pictures printed."

Amy giggled. "And you didn't think anyone would be interested. When you bring in your negatives, we'll check my own stock; I could probably use some more myself."

A few miles north of Fort Bragg, Paul pulled off the highway and parked in front of a restaurant with a huge neon flower over the door.

"The Purple Rose? Wonderful!" Amy declared. "I haven't been here in ages. You're going to love this," she said, turning to Beth. "They have the best fish tacos."

"Fish tacos?" Beth made a face.

"I know what you're thinking," Tom said. "I felt the same way the first time someone mentioned them to me. Growing up in Indiana, I'd never heard of such a thing.

And of course the image of a small brook trout wrapped in a tortilla didn't help."

"Oh, Tom. Give it a rest." Amy turned to Beth. "Actually the fish consists of these delicate morsels, battered and fried to a golden brown and then topped with shredded cabbage, pico de gallo, and aioli. Yummy!"

A few minutes later, the four of them were seated at a table. Amy had never seen the place so packed with people, laughing and talking, having a great time.

"Let's start with a pitcher of margaritas," Paul suggested when the waitress came to take their order.

"Don't forget the taquitos and guacamole," Amy added, peering at him over her menu.

"So, how was your visit to the Botanical Gardens?" Tom asked as they waited for their drinks and appetizers.

"Grace and Charlie had a record crowd this year. I think they had every artist in northern California there, not to mention all the wineries. And the baskets Grace put together were scrumptious, weren't they Beth?"

"Everything was wonderful. The wine was good and the artistry was amazing. I'd never seen so many beautiful pieces before."

"And she wants to go back and photograph the flowers," Amy said, smiling at Beth as she began filling her glass from the margarita pitcher that had just arrived. "So, I was thinking..."

"I'd be happy to take you," Paul interjected, "unless you've made other plans."

"Well, we hadn't planned anything yet, but..." Beth hesitated.

Amy stopped pouring the frozen beverage and looked up to find three pairs of eyes staring at her. "What?"

"Paul's offered to take me to the Botanical Gardens, that is, if you don't mind."

Amy finished serving herself and took a huge sip. "Mind?" *Which part? The part where Paul will be taking you in my place or the part where you will be spending time with Paul.* "Don't be silly." She gave everyone a big smile. "Why would I mind?"

"Great!" Paul said. "I can slip away late Monday morning if that's okay with you, Beth."

"Sure, and that'll give me a few days to get more photo cards done. I still can't believe they're selling so well."

"Oh, speaking of selling," Amy began, dipping a taquito in the guacamole. "I finally sold some of those Black Sapphire products Sandy convinced me to buy."

"To a local or someone passing through?" Tom asked as he took a turn filling his own glass with the ice cold margarita mixture.

"Neither. I'd put them on the website, and some woman from L.A. ordered one of the love potions as well as a vial of patchouli oil."

"I didn't think people wore patchouli anymore," Paul said. "I mean, my mom used to but that was years ago."

"My old girlfriend, Debra Osborn, used to wear it," Tom offered, swirling a taquito in the guacamole.

Amy stared at him. "Omigod, that's the name."

"Name of what?" he asked around the mouthful of food.

"The woman that ordered the stuff."

"Isn't that strange?" Beth said, as Tom began to choke. "Oh dear! Are you all right?"

Paul reached over and clapped him on the back a couple of times. "You okay?"

Tom held up his hand and nodded. By the time he'd grabbed his glass of water and had a sip, he was breathing again.

Tom Miller poured a third glass of his favorite cabernet sauvignon through the aerator and settled onto the sofa but this new location offered no more of a distraction than the others. He'd tried reading in his recliner, sitting at the computer checking out the latest news, and even standing before the large bay windows staring out over the water. Nothing worked; he couldn't get what Amy had said earlier that evening out of his mind. Looking at the large wall space between the matching windows, he realized he may just have to rethink the whole television thing.

What is Debra up to, and why is she involving people in Mendocino?

A sharp, stabbing pain developed behind his left eye, so he drained his glass and laid his head back on the sofa. The throbbing had begun to subside when the email signal on his computer sounded. Hoping the incoming message would provide the diversion he was looking for, he pushed himself up and wandered over to his desk. He was wrong. Instead, it brought the problem fully into focus. It was from Debra. "What the hell!" The pain returned, this time behind both eyes, and his pulse pounded in his head. He clicked on the message, half-expecting his computer to explode. "Haven't heard from you," it began, "so I hope everything is okay. Just wanted you to know I'm sending something I'm sure you'll just love." Tom seriously doubted it as he deleted her message. How was he going to get this lunatic to leave him alone? Carmine Scaglione's help was looking better and better.

CHAPTER 14

"Well, Annie, I've checked this camera bag three times," Beth Braddock told the old dog as she zipped it closed again. "I must be a little nervous." She opened the door just as Paul pulled up in front of the house. "There he is. Come on, let's get you chained up." But the dog did not move from her spot in front of the fridge. Instead, she placed her head on her paws and whimpered.

"Hey Annie," the man said as he stepped through the open front door. "Look what I have." He held up a large rawhide bone and wiggled it at her. "It's gravy flavored."

With her ears at full attention, the dog got to her feet and followed Paul out to the water tank where he secured the chain to her collar and gave her the bone. "There you go, Girl," he said, patting her head. Annie lay down and immediately began the arduous task of reducing the giant bone to a small, soggy lump.

"That was a great idea," Beth said when he joined her at the bottom of the steps. "I thought I was going to have to carry her outside."

"All in a day's work. Here, let me take that for you." Paul took Beth's camera bag, put it in the back of his car, and opened the passenger side door for her. After she was settled, he slid in behind the wheel and started the car.

"I'm afraid it's going to be overcast today," he said, pulling away from the curb.

"Actually, the colors will be more vivid if it is. The bright sun tends to fade them."

"Really? I didn't know that. Then the day should be perfect all around."

Stealing a sideways glance, Beth marveled at how handsome the man was, with his square chin and the chiseled jaw. Being sensitive and charming too, he reminded her of Tony except...

"Everything okay?" he asked.

Beth had been staring at Paul again, and he'd caught her. "No, I mean yes." She felt her face grow hot. He smiled, and she couldn't help smiling back. *Yes, it should be a perfect day.*

They rode the rest of the way in silence until Paul pulled into the parking lot at the Botanical Gardens. Unlike the other day when she'd come with Amy, there were only two other cars parked there.

"Looks like we've got the place to ourselves," Paul said as he climbed out of the Honda. He stepped around the front of the small SUV, opened the door for Beth, and then moved to the back of the vehicle.

"Will you be locking your car?" Beth asked. "I'd like to leave my purse here, so I don't have to pack it around."

"Sure. Let me get my stuff together, and we can get started." He wrestled out a large backpack that made a strange clunking sound as he swung it onto his back. Then he grabbed Beth's camera bag and handed it to her. Last to come out was a large sketchpad.

"You sketch?"

"Oh, I tinker with it. Thought it would be a great way to pass the time while you take pictures. Okay, I think I'm ready. Let's go." Paul started to shut the door and then stopped. "Oh, I almost forgot." He reached back inside and took out a small box, opened it and put a silver packet in his shirt pocket. When he tossed the box back into the car, she saw it was a disposable camera. Paul smiled at her sheepishly but didn't say anything.

After they picked a spot with a central location, Beth unpacked her camera and attached the autowind. With her extra lenses and filters tucked in her jacket pocket, she left her camera bag with Paul and was soon totally engrossed in her photography, experimenting with composition and depth of field. Each time she glanced his way, he was busily sketching on his pad and seemed to be having as much fun as she was. When she could no longer ignore her rumbling stomach, she walked over and sat down next to him.

"Did you get all the pictures you wanted?" he asked, closing his sketchpad.

"I think so." Beth disassembled her camera and re-packed all her photography equipment back into her bag. "And I'm starving."

Paul stood and slipped his left arm through one of the straps on his backpack. "Then come with me." He led the way down the North Trail. A few minutes later, they came to a wooded area, turned right, and followed a narrow path to a small building that looked out over the ocean. Inside, whalebones hung on one wall and photographs of the coastal area were on another. "This is the Cliff House. Isn't it great?" he asked, guiding her over to one of the benches. As she sat down, he took off his backpack and stood it in front of her. "Hold this would you, so I can un-pack our lunch."

"Lunch?" Beth asked, grasping the backpack and balancing it in front of her.

The first thing to come out was a red and white checked

tablecloth, which Paul spread on the bench next to her. Then he took out a bottle of wine and two glasses followed by a small jar of olives, a brick of Havarti cheese, and a package of sourdough crackers. A couple of apples and a handful of mint chocolates completed the meal. From the outside pocket, he pulled out a knife and corkscrew and laid them next to the bottle of wine. "There we are."

Beth's stomach grumbled again.

"My, you are hungry," Paul chuckled. "Let's dig in."

The basket she'd shared with Amy was delicious but the coziness of the cliff house and the rhythmic murmur of the waves caressing the rocks made sharing this picnic much more romantic. Halfway through the meal, the first wisps of a fog bank began to blow by.

"Look at that. I think I have a couple of pictures left, and that'll make a great shot." Beth grabbed her camera, snapped on a lens, and walked over to the large plate glass window that looked out over the ocean.

Paul moved in next to her and leaned on the railing in front of the window. After taking a couple pictures, Beth realized he was there.

"What is it?" she asked, aware he was staring at her. Without a word, he bent down and kissed her tenderly on the lips.

"Oh!" She stepped back. "What — what'd you do that for?" Beth retreated to the bench and stuffed the camera back into the bag. "I think we'd better go now." She stood and threw the strap over her shoulder, but Paul blocked her way when she tried to leave.

"Beth, I'm sorry." He reached out but did not touch her. "I didn't mean to startle you."

"It's just...well, I mean...I feel like I'm being unfaithful." Tears filled her dark brown eyes and trickled down her cheeks.

Caressing her head with his hands, Paul gently wiped away her tears with his thumbs. "I didn't mean to upset you. I just thought —"

Beth pushed him away. "I appreciate what you've done. Today was truly wonderful. I just don't think I'm ready for any kind of relationship other than friendship. I hope you understand."

"It won't happen again; I promise. It just hard because I find myself caring about you." He stepped back over to the bench. "Give me a second to pack this up and then we can head back."

Beth nodded and watched as he returned the remnants of the romantic lunch to the backpack.

CHAPTER 15

I t wasn't until the third ring that Beth Braddock realized the phone in her dream was actually her own. She threw back the covers and stumbled out to the kitchen, barely able to see in the predawn light. "Hello?"

"Beth?"

"Yes?"

"It's Paul. I'm sorry to call so early, but I'm in kind of a bind and was hoping you might be willing to give me a hand."

She hadn't seen or talked to him for almost a week, not since he'd taken her to the Botanical Gardens. But given the hour of the call, she assumed it was something important. "Sure, if I can."

"I'm sold out, and Clara is not feeling well. I could sure use your help with breakfast and the housekeeping this morning."

"Oh dear. Is she all right?" Although the short, white-haired woman had initially scared the crap out of her, Beth hated the idea that she might be ill.

"Yeah, I'm sure it's just some twenty-four hour bug, but she's out of commission for the day." He paused. "So, what do you say?"

"Um, well...what time should I be there?" She squinted at the clock on the stove. Half past five.

"Well, I need to have the tables set and breakfast ready

for twenty people by seven o'clock, so as soon as possible would be great."

"Okay. What should I wear?"

"We're pretty relaxed on dress code, so wear whatever you'd like. See you soon."

With no time to fuss over hair or make-up, Beth threw on a pair of black jeans and a fuchsia T-shirt with a scoop neck and cap sleeves. After tugging on her tennis shoes, she stepped into the bathroom and swept her hair up into a ponytail. "Okay Annie, time to get up," she said as she hurried past the bed where the old dog remained spread out on her side. Beth pulled on her buffalo-plaid jacket and opened the front door. "Come on, girl." She patted the side of her leg a couple of times, and reluctantly Annie left her warm spot and joined her master at the door. "We'll go for our romp when I get back," Beth told the dog as she hooked the chain to the dog's collar and gave her ears a vigorous scratching. After making sure Annie's water dish was full, she headed for the bed & breakfast.

It was strangely quiet when Beth opened the front door and tiptoed through the dining room. Pushing the swinging door open, she stepped into the kitchen. "Paul?"

"Hang on, be right there," he called from somewhere out of view.

As Beth waited for Paul to appear, she marveled at the spotless kitchen. A stainless steel worktable that served as an island dominated the room. An assortment of sauce and frying pans hung from the matching rack directly above it. Metal bowls and pots arranged by size filled the shelf underneath and a complete selection of cooking utensils dangled from a rack on one end. As she moved toward the sink, Paul's sudden appearance through a door she hadn't noticed next to the refrigerator made her jump. "Oh!" she exclaimed.

"Sorry, didn't mean to startle you. I was getting the fruit and eggs out of the cool room."

"Cool room?"

"Yeah, it's a small, sunken room lined with river rock cemented into place," he said, pointing with his elbow back the way he'd come. "It was the only way to keep things cold when this place was originally built." He dumped his load on the stainless table. "I really appreciate you coming to help. Let me show you where the glasses and utensils are, and you can start setting the tables."

"Sure." Beth shrugged out of her jacket. "Where should I put this?" she asked.

"Here," Paul said, taking it. "We'll put it on the back of the door next to mine." He exchanged her jacket for the short, white apron hanging on the hook. "This is an extra you can use," he said, handing it over. Then he took her into the dining room and showed her where the tablecloths, dishes, and utensils were stored and how to set the tables. "As soon as you're done, come back into the kitchen, and you can help me finish up."

"Okay." Beth slipped the apron over her head and tied it around her waist. Then she quickly finished setting the table Paul had started. Shaking out the remaining tablecloths and placing them on the other tables, she realized she was humming. It felt good to be doing something productive; a feeling she hadn't had for sometime, even when she was making her photo cards. She'd just finished with the large oval table when a loud crash came from the kitchen.

"Dammit!" Paul exclaimed.

"Are you all right?" Beth called.

"Yeah, just bumped my mixing bowl off the counter."

"Need help?"

"Crap! No, I got it." Paul chuckled. "I'll just have to whip up the eggs for the French toast again."

Beth giggled and immediately felt bad for doing so. She doubled her efforts and had the dining room ready to receive hungry guests in a few minutes. Then she pushed through the swinging door and back into the kitchen. "What would you like me to do now?" she asked, noticing a wad of paper towels coated in egg goo partially shoved under the table.

Paul was pulling handfuls of bacon out of a box and arranging them on a large baking sheet. "Let's see, you can wash those strawberries," he said pointing to the large flat of berries he'd brought out of the cool room. "There's a colander on the shelf underneath them. Just watch out for the mess on the floor."

"Okay." Beth watched him for a moment. "I don't claim to know much about cooking, but shouldn't you have parchment paper under those, so they don't stick?"

He stopped, bacon dangling from both hands. "Ugh, you're right. I forgot it." He plopped the breakfast meat back into its box and stepped over to a gigantic cupboard next to the door. Beth cringed as he pulled the doors open with his greasy hands. "It should be in here." He rummaged around and soon located it. "I should've had this in the oven ten minutes ago," he began, moving back over to the stove, "but now I have to start over."

Beth looked at the baking sheet almost completely covered with the sliced bacon. "Not necessarily." She moved over next to him and took the roll of parchment paper. "If we put the paper on top like this..." She tore off a piece and placed it over the bacon. "Then grab another baking sheet and turn it over on top, like this," she said, following her own directions, "flip it over and..." She laughed after separating the baking sheets. "Well, most of the slices fell off."

"I knew it was a good idea to ask you to help." Paul beamed at her. "Thanks." He peeled off the few slices still stuck to the pan and added them to the one lined with paper. Then, as Beth rinsed the strawberries, he finished loading both pans with bacon and slid them into the restaurant-style oven. "There are a couple of cantaloupes in the cool room, if you wouldn't mind getting them, and I'll fetch the platter for the fruit."

Beth stepped over to the open doorway where Paul had suddenly appeared and was surprised at the change in temperature as she followed the wooden steps into the low-ceilinged subterranean room. About the size of a small walk-in closet, it was lined with wooden shelves worn smooth by years of use. They held all kinds of fresh fruit and vegetables, as well as a selection of cheeses. Rows of Mason jars containing home canned tomatoes, green beans, peaches, and cherries along with smaller jars filled with jewel-colored jams and jellies covered the top shelves.

"Did you find them?"

"Huh?" Beth quickly glanced around. "Got 'em," she said, snagging two of the melons and hurrying back up the stairs. "Sorry, I was admiring all the canned food. Is that Clara's handiwork?"

"Yes," he chuckled, "she has been doing that for as long as I can remember." He finished filling a tall, metal coffee pot with water and pulled it out of the sink. "After I get the coffee started, I'll get the French toast going, if you'll cut up fruit and arrange it on the platter I set out." He replaced the basket, added several scoops of coffee and slid the lid into place.

By the time Beth had the fruit ready to serve, the smell of cinnamon, bacon, and fresh-brewed coffee filled the kitchen. Her stomach growled loudly as she and Paul carried the food into the dining room, just as the first of the guests wandered in. For the next two hours, they refilled coffee cups and juice glasses, cleared tables, and served an occasional latte. Paul even had to excuse himself a couple of times to help some guests who wanted to checkout early. When the dining room was finally empty, the two of them dropped into the nearest chairs.

"Oh my," Beth exclaimed, fanning herself with the hem of her apron. "That was quite an ordeal. How did Clara manage after your mother became ill?"

"She didn't have to. Mom had already hired a gal named Belinda Johnson to work part-time. She was awesome and assumed most of the responsibility when Mom got sick."

"She doesn't help out any more?"

Paul laughed. "When she found out I was coming home, she quit and married the man she'd met here last year. It's just me and Clara now."

"Is it this hectic every morning?"

"This is only the second time we've been completely sold out since I got back. And with Clara in the kitchen, there's a lot less chaos."

Just then the back door slammed shut. "What on earth have you done to my kitchen?"

Paul exploded out of the chair, his eyes wide-open. "Clara!" he exclaimed in a stage-like whisper. He hurried through the swinging door, Beth close behind him. "Should you be out of bed?" he asked the short cook who was wearing a quilted pink robe and matching slippers.

"I ran out of orange juice and came to get some." She looked around and placed her hands on her hips. "Paul Michael Hayden, what have you done to my kitchen?" she demanded.

"I just had a little trouble with a few things. I'll get it cleaned up, I promise."

Shaking her head, she shuffled over to the fridge, pulled out a partial container of juice, and hugged it to her chest. "Well, see that you do." Then she disappeared through the back door.

"Oh my," Beth sighed. "She was not happy with you."

"Yeah," Paul said, pinching the bridge of his nose. "She considers this her territory — and she expects it to be kept clean." He ran his right hand through his wavy hair as he surveyed the damage. "To be honest, she took it better than I anticipated, which means she might be sicker than I thought." He smiled at Beth. "Ready to dive in?"

"Sure, but..." Beth shifted her gaze from the stainless table piled with greasy baking sheets, mixing bowls, bread wrappers, and gooey cooking utensils to the sink filled with dirty dishes. "...where do we begin?"

"Let's start with the dishes in the dining room. I'll work on what's in the sink, if you want to bring the rest in." He grabbed a large, grey rectangular tub from under the sink and handed it to Beth. She pushed back through the swinging door and began clearing tables. By the time she took her first load into the kitchen, Paul had the sink cleared and the dishwasher going.

"As soon as we have this mucked out," he said, grinning as he swapped her full tub for an empty one, "we'll get started on the rooms."

Paul Hayden grabbed the last pile of linens that had been stripped from the beds upstairs and thrown down next to the lobby on the first floor. Starting on the downstairs rooms off the large porch of the bed & breakfast, he and Beth had systematically cleaned each room. After changing the beds together, she dusted and vacuumed while he scrubbed down the bathrooms and hung clean towels. Two and a half hours later, the rooms were done and the place was void of all guests.

"Last batch," he said, dropping the armload of soiled laundry next to the large-capacity washing machine.

"Thank goodness." Beth stopped folding the hot, fluffy towels that had just been removed from the dryer long enough to wipe a strand of hair from her sweaty face. "My arms are about ready to fall off."

He laughed. "Come on," he said, taking her hand and leading her to the kitchen. "Let's make a couple of BLT sandwiches, and I think there's some of Clara's sweet tea to go with them. We can have lunch out on the porch. I'll finish the rest of this later." Keeping the mess to a minimum, they prepared a simple lunch of sandwiches and sliced fruit leftover from breakfast and carried it out to the porch swing that hung from the support beam.

"Thanks again," Paul said after they'd eaten for several minutes in silence. "I'm sure I'd still be trying to clean up the breakfast mess."

"You're welcome." Beth smiled at him. "I actually enjoyed helping out." She studied the strawberry slices still on her plate as she poked at them with her finger. "I wouldn't mind helping out again sometime."

"Really? It did go quicker with your help and was definitely more fun." He stared at her until she looked up at him and then gave her a huge smile, which she immediately returned.

"What kind of tree is that?" she asked, breaking the brief awkwardness that followed.

"That is a holly tree. When my great-aunt Lucile bought this place in 1906, she planted it to ward off evil."

"Ward off evil?"

Paul nodded. "Apparently, she was quite eccentric and planting the tree was supposed to protect her from lightning, sickness, and witchcraft."

"Did it work?"

"Well, she lived for almost ninety-three years and was never sick a day in her life. To my knowledge this place has never been hit by lightning, but I can't say for sure whether or not a witch has stayed here. Not usually the kind of question you ask when someone is checking in."

Beth giggled. "Sounds like it did what it's supposed to."

"Yeah, but it's getting out of hand. I don't think Mom ever pruned it, and now it's practically shrouded the entire bed & breakfast." He shook his head. "I really should whack it way back. It would open up the front yard and look so much better."

Beth tipped her head to one side and stared at the unruly tree for awhile. Finally, she turned back to him. "Maybe there's a reason why she never trimmed it. What if cutting its branches is bad luck? You know, like breaking a mirror."

"Oh come on," Paul chuckled. "Bad luck? Really?"

Beth shrugged her shoulders and giggled again. "Just a suggestion as to why no one ever trimmed it. Was your mom superstitious?"

"She was no more superstitious than I am." He had to admit it was strange, though. His mother had been particular about her rose bushes. They had to be meticulously pruned and weeds kept at bay, but he couldn't remember a single time when he'd seen her even come close to the holly tree with clippers in her hand. Maybe there was a reason why Margaret Hayden allowed it to grow unchecked. Maybe...

"Paul?"

"Huh?" He blinked at Beth while his thoughts returned to the present.

"What's got you so preoccupied?

He smiled. "Oh, nothing. More tea?"

CHAPTER 16

Paul Hayden pulled in behind Tom's Z3 and cut the motor. When Amy had mentioned she and Tom were coming to Fort Bragg, he suggested the four of them meet at Egghead's for an early breakfast. It was a perfect opportunity to spend time with Beth other than cleaning at the bed & breakfast and without the formality of being on a date. "Here we are," he said, grinning at her.

She looked out her window at the row of businesses lining the street. "It looks so small."

"It is, but they've made very good use of every inch of space." He joined Beth on the sidewalk. "This was my mother's favorite restaurant. We ate here every time we came to Fort Bragg."

"Why did she like it so much?"

"I can't tell you without spoiling the surprise. Come on." He stepped over to the door and held it open.

"Oh my goodness," Beth said as she stepped inside.

Paul chuckled as he moved in behind her. The place was just how he'd remembered it. Photographs and billboards from the *Wizard of Oz* hung wherever there was a space big enough, and black and white checkered tiles covered the floor. Vintage wooden booths lined one wall and small tables, barely big enough for two, were arranged along the other under a huge mural of the famous foursome standing on the yellow brick road just outside the

Emerald City. The aroma of garlicky fried potatoes and sizzling bacon wafted from the kitchen, bringing with it a feeling of familiarity.

"My mother was a huge Judy Garland fan," Paul said, leaning in closer. "That's why she loved to come here so much. That and the food."

Amy leaned around the high back of a booth at the back of the restaurant and waved. "About time you two got here," she called, scooting over to make room for Beth on her bench. "I'm starving."

"What else is new?" Tom said as Paul slid in next to him.

"Don't even start with me, Tom Miller," Amy replied from behind her menu. "I told you I didn't get a chance to eat anything before we left, and when my blood sugar gets low, I just can't function."

Beth glanced at Paul and smiled; he winked back. "So what's good here?" she asked, picking up a menu and looking at it.

"Just about everything," Tom replied. "My personal favorite is Toto's Treat. An omelet full of ham, bacon, and sausage. No vegetables to get in the way."

"Dorothy's Delight sounds good," Beth said. "Spinach, mushrooms, cream cheese, and bacon."

"I have a hard time choosing between it and the Scarecrow Scramble. It's full of taco meat, tomatoes, and cheese," Amy said.

"I'll have the steak and eggs," Paul told the waitress who'd just arrived with two more mugs of steaming coffee. When he was younger, his mother only let him order that on special occasions. Smiling at Beth across the table, he didn't think his mother would object.

Tom gave his order, and Beth did the same. Then everyone stared at Amy, waiting.

"I know, I know, but I just can't decide," Amy wailed.

"Why don't you get the scramble and we'll share," Beth suggested. "That way we both get some of each one."

"Grand idea," Amy said, relinquishing her menu. "Now then, what have you two been up to?"

"Us?" Beth glanced at Paul.

"*WE* haven't been doing anything — I, on the other hand, have been busy keeping Clara happy at the bed & breakfast. The only break I've gotten lately is going to my writing class." Paul turned to his breakfast companion and smiled. "How about you? What have you been up to?"

"Uh well, when I'm not helping out at the bed & breakfast," Beth said, smiling back at him, "I'm filling orders for my photo cards. It seems I get a call every day from someone to bring more."

"Didn't you take pictures at the Botanical Gardens?" Tom asked.

"Yes, I did."

Amy reached for a package of saltines and tore them open. "How did they turn out? Sandy developed them, and I didn't get a chance to see them before you picked them up."

"Apparently, I forgot how to use my magnifying lens, so some of them are out of focus. Otherwise, I think they turned out okay."

"Well, I'd love to see them. Remember I mentioned I've been looking for pictures of flowers to hang in my sunroom. If they're as good as your other photographs, I know they'll be perfect." Amy finished off the saltines she'd been nibbling. "Now, tell us about this writing class," she said, turning to Paul.

"Well, it's going to be great if it doesn't get cancelled."

Amy frowned at him. "Why would it get cancelled?"

"Seems the college needs to have a certain number

of students enrolled in the evening classes to keep them open. Right now we're short four people. In fact, I was going to ask if any of you would like to come next week."

"Sorry chum, not me," Tom said. "I collect books; I don't write them."

"I wouldn't mind giving it a try. What night is it?" Amy asked, reaching for another package of crackers.

"Wednesdays, at seven o'clock."

"Ooh, that's my yoga night. Sorry. What about you Beth?"

"Oh, I haven't written for a long time," Beth said shaking her head. "I don't think I'd remember how."

Paul slid his foot across the floor until it made contact with Beth's. "Why don't you come to class with me next Wednesday and see if you like it?" he suggested. "You wouldn't have to register beforehand."

Beth stared at him with her deep, brown eyes. The same brown eyes that had pleaded with him that day in the Cliff House. "I'll think about it and let you know Wednesday morning," she offered.

Paul smiled. "Fair enough."

"So what exactly brought you to Fort Bragg this early in the morning?" Beth asked Tom.

"Molly, over at the Paul Bunyan Thrift Shop got in a huge donation from an estate sale that included several boxes of old books. Since she knows I'm a collector, she called me right away."

"Was there anything valuable?" Paul asked, pouring cream from a small silver pitcher into his coffee.

Before Tom could answer, the waitress set plates down in front of both of them, a mountain of fried potatoes piled on each one. "Now that's what I call a breakfast," he exclaimed, rubbing his hands together.

Paul waited while Tom topped his omelet with hot

sauce, spread jelly on his toast, and took his first bite. Then, as he cut into his own plump, juicy steak with a large serrated knife, he asked his question again. "So did you?"

Tom held up a finger as he washed down his bite with a sip of coffee. "Did I what?"

Paul glanced at the two women sitting across from him and rolled his eyes. "Find anything valuable?"

Tom shook his head as he cut another chunk off his omelet. "There were a few older first editions; nothing that interested me, but I gave Molly the name of a reliable broker. She should make somewhere around a thousand dollars on those particular books. The rest were just yard sale quality."

The waitress returned with two more plates and placed them on the table.

"Finally," Amy exclaimed as she pulled her napkin from underneath her silverware and spread it across her lap. "I was getting lightheaded." Using her knife, she divided her scramble in half. "Here, use this to cut yours and then we'll switch." Beth obeyed, and the group fell silent as attentions shifted from conversation to eggs and potatoes.

The trip north was quiet Wednesday evening as Paul's Honda Element sped toward Fort Bragg. Doubts plagued Beth Braddock's mind. *Why did I agree to go with him?* Writing had always conjured up old memories, and she wasn't ready for that. Not yet. Maybe it would be all right if she just focused on Paul and the time she'd be spending with him.

"Almost there," he said, looking over at Beth and smiling. "I'm so glad you finally agreed to come with me. It's always more fun to take a class with someone you know."

"To be honest, I am feeling a little nervous."

Paul chuckled. "Don't be. I just appreciate the fact that you're willing to give it a try. If you don't like it, it's no big deal. Besides, it gives us a chance to get to know one another while we travel back and forth."

Doubt turned to panic. *What did he mean by that?* Maybe she should insist he turn the car around right now. It's not too late to change her mind. Maybe she should say she's not feeling well. Maybe...

"The class is over here to the right," Paul said, pointing to a small modular building as he maneuvered into the college parking lot. "During the break we'll go to the little cafeteria and get some coffee." He pulled into the nearest parking space, and the two of them got out. Beth followed him into a small classroom occupied by a dozen people of various ages. "See a place you like?" he asked.

"Toward the back, if you don't mind," she whispered, hugging her things close to her chest.

"That's my usual spot. You can sit here, and I'll squeeze in next to you." He dropped his books onto the desk and held out his hand. "Give me your coat and I'll put it with mine."

Reluctantly, Beth shrugged out of her buffalo-plaid jacket and passed it over.

Paul slipped off his own leather jacket and hung both on the back of a nearby vacant chair. He'd just settled in his own chair when an older woman swept into the room, her permed salt and pepper hair cut into a bobbed hairstyle. The chiffon scarf she wore around her neck flowed when she moved, as did her floral skirt and blouse. "Good evening class. How is everyone?" she asked, dumping the oversized patchwork bag she'd had slung on one shoulder into a chair next to her. Without waiting for a reply, she continued. "Well, how do our numbers look tonight?" She glanced around the room, counting to herself. "Terrific, we should have enough now to keep the class going. Have all of you registered?" Most nodded their heads. "Who hasn't?" Beth raised her hand along with an older gentleman and a girl who looked to be twelve. "You'll need to register by Friday so we can get your names on the roster before the census. In fact," she said, pulling a small bundle out of her bag, "I have enrollment cards with me that you can fill out and drop by the office between eight and five." She dropped them on a corner of the large table in front of her.

"Now, let's get started. Tonight I would like to discuss poetry and to get us started let's focus on what it's like to lose someone close to us. Let your emotions go. Write the first thing that comes to mind. Don't worry about form..."

As the instructor continued to speak, Beth looked over at Paul. He was looking right at her, a grimace on his face. "Sorry," he mouthed. Beth almost laughed out loud. Almost. Poor Paul. She was sure he felt terrible, and she shrugged her shoulders at him.

"So, now that we know what we're writing about, begin."

With a sigh, Beth flipped open her new notebook and stared at the blank page. Where to start? After jotting a few notes she wrote:

Side by side, we made our way
Played together, learned from each other
Explored who we really were.

Side by side, we built our home
Talked of increasing our number
Begin the journey of family.

Without warning you went away
Never again to be by my side.
Was it your wish to go?

Gone are your laughing eyes,
Your broad smile, warm embrace.
How lonely our bed has become.

Each day I wait for your return
Always searching the crowd for your face,
I understand I must be patient.

Counting the days, the minutes, the hours,
Hoping there will not be too many
Until we are again, side by side.

She looked at the poem in astonishment; it was as if someone else had written it. As she read through it, she could feel the heat spreading behind her eyes. She had to get out of the tiny room.

Beth closed her notebook and stood. "I have to get some air," she whispered to Paul as she snatched her jacket from the chair. Hurrying from the classroom, tears formed in her eyes, making it difficult to see where she was going. Finally, she found the outer door and collapsed onto the first bench she came across.

"Get a grip," she told herself. "It was just a poem." But the tears continued. "Oh, this is ridiculous!" As she wiped at her face with her sleeve, a hand rested on her shoulder.

"Are you okay?" Paul asked, moving around the bench and sitting next to her.

"Yes, just being hormonal. I hope I didn't embarrass you too much."

"Not at all. Shall I get our stuff and take you home?"

"Don't be silly. I'll be all right. Just give me another minute to get myself together."

"Are you're sure? I had no idea she was going to do that or I wouldn't have asked you to come."

"It's okay, really." Beth took a deep breath. "I think I'm ready to go back inside."

"Well then..." Paul stood and grandly swept his hands toward the door. "After you."

Quietly the pair slipped back into the classroom. Beth reopened her notebook and turned to a clean page.

"Now let's take a look at another aspect of loss," the instructor said, scribbling on the white board behind her. "Religious beliefs. Most of us have some kind of belief system. How has loss affected that? Ready, write."

Again Beth looked at the blank page before her. But this time, without hesitation she penned:

I followed Your teachings
Tried to do as You said.
But You took him.

I told others of You
Tried to spread Your word.
But You took him.

Now I am alone.
No more song in my life
Because You took him.

You took him away, now
I long to follow him.
But I am afraid — of YOU.

At the end of the last line, Beth stabbed the paper with so much force her pencil point broke. Her eyes darted about the room but no one else seemed to notice, not even Paul. Again Beth closed her notebook but there were no tears this time. In fact, Beth had to slow her breathing down; she was practically panting.

CHAPTER 17

The third time the power went out, Amy Thompson had had enough. Without electricity, the gift shop would grow cold quickly and she wasn't about to freeze. Turning on the flashlight she'd slipped into her pocket the first time the lights flickered, she made her way to the phone and dialed Beth's number. Huddled in front of her massive fireplace was the best place to endure such a storm and her friend might want to join her. But when Beth didn't answer by the seventh ring, she hung up. Anxious to get home before it got any worse, Amy grabbed her bag, flicked all the light switches to the off position and headed for the front door. Just as she reached out to open it, the phone rang.

Hoping it might be Beth, Amy stumbled toward the back in the near dark and reached it before it stopped ringing. "Hello?"

"Amy?"

"Yes..." She wasn't sure she recognized the voice.

"It's Paul."

"Oh hey, what's up?"

"Have you seen Beth? I can't seem to get her on the phone." His voice sounded strained.

"I just tried to call her myself. She's probably still out taking photographs. I talked to her this morning as the storm was rolling in, and she told me she wanted to get some pictures before it got too bad."

"Do you know where she was going?"

"I'm not sure. She may have mentioned something about the headland."

"The headland?" he shouted.

Before Amy could reply, she heard a click and then nothing. "And good-bye to you too," she said, holding the receiver out in front of her.

Beth Braddock couldn't believe what terrific shots she was getting. The ocean seemed alive, undulating and swirling below her. Four times massive waves had hit the rocks, sending huge walls of spray into the air. She hoped the film in her camera was fast enough to capture them in the subdued lighting. The clouds above her were so dark; it was like they were sucking away the light of day.

She turned around and watched her chocolate lab pace back and forth on the ledge above her. Try as she might, she could not coax the dog any closer to the water. Annie just moved first one direction and then the other, barking at Beth the whole time.

"You really are a silly dog," she called, turning back to the open water. She could see a wave, much larger than the others, moving toward shore. *This is going to be spectacular.* Beth raised the camera to her eye and waited. Just as she held her breath to click the shutter, a hand grabbed her by the arm and spun her around. Startled, she screamed and found herself face-to-face with Paul.

"What the hell are you doing?" he demanded. His rain-soaked hair hung down in his face and his green eyes blazed. Beth was so frightened, she stepped back quickly and almost lost her footing. Paul grabbed her by the shoulders and shook her. "Don't you realize how danger-ous this is?" he shouted above the roar of the waves, caus-ing Annie to jump down from the ledge and charge at him, a low growl coming from deep within her.

"What is wrong with you?" Beth yelled, pulling away from him. "You scared me to death!" She turned and scrambled up the steep path. Annie joined her on the trail, and before the two of them had gone very far, a torrential rain poured from the dark clouds.

Paul continued shouting, but she couldn't make out what he was saying. Looking behind her, Beth saw him running up the trail toward her, his yellow rain slicker whipped about by the wind. She began to run, but before she could reach the break in the fence, Paul jumped in front of her and blocked her way.

"Look, I'm sorry I frightened you," he said, grabbing hold of her again, "but you scared me. When I saw you standing on that narrow ledge with that wave bearing down on you, all I could think of was getting to you before it did. I'm sorry. I shouldn't have yelled at you. Come back to the bed & breakfast with me; we're getting soaked."

Beth shook her head. "I just don't understand why you're so upset."

"I know you don't, and I'll explain it to you when we get there."

"Why don't we go to my place? It's closer," Beth said, looking in the direction of her house.

"The power's out, and I'll be willing to bet your house is freezing. I've started a fire at my place, and we'll be warmer there. Come on, Beth. Please."

"All right, but let me get some dry clothes first." She turned and hurried across the street.

Paul followed her up the front steps and waited on the porch while she stuffed a few things into a small bag. By the time they'd reached the bed & breakfast, all three of them were drenched, and Beth was so cold her teeth were chattering.

"Come on, you can change in my room," Paul said, escorting her up the stairs. At the top of the stairway, he turned left and opened one of the doors at the end of the short hallway. "I'll go change downstairs," he said, grabbing some clothes out of his dresser. "When you're ready, meet me by the fireplace and I'll explain." With that, he stepped into the hall and closed the door behind him.

Beth moved into the adjoining bathroom, peeled off her wet clothes, and tossed everything into the antique bathtub. After drying off with one of Paul's towels, she put on the dry clothes she'd grabbed and walked back into the bedroom. As she finished toweling her hair, she looked around.

The polished brass bed dominated the room, and the area rug beneath it revealed hardwood floors buffed to a high gloss. A large trunk sat at the end of the bed, and Beth carefully lifted the lid. Inside were several quilts, each one made from colorful swatches of material. A familiar, musty smell drifted up to her nose and swept her back in time to her grandmother's house where countless nights had been spent under blankets and quilts with a similar scent. Closing the trunk, she noticed the heavy curtains hanging over the windows, each one pulled back into a solid brass tieback. Underneath, ivory sheers gave the view outside a dreamy appearance.

An antique dresser that was taller than Beth loomed in one corner, and a marble-topped washstand and matching settee were nestled in another. Stepping closer to the washstand, she noticed two pictures hanging on the wall behind it. The black and white photograph had obviously been taken several years ago, but there was no mistaking the resemblance between Paul and the man in the photo. He had on a peasant shirt that was open at the neck, and the woman standing beside him wore a simple white dress and a halo of flowers in her hair. The other photo was in color and had been taken more recently in front of the bed & breakfast. The woman was much older and, although she was smiling, looked sad somehow. A happy, younger version of Paul with shoulder length hair, stood next to her, his arm draped across her shoulders.

The only modern furniture in the room was the drafting table placed in front of the windows. On it were several sketch pads, a computer, and what must have been manuscripts from his writing class. Moving closer, Beth peeked inside one of the pads and was shocked to find sketches of herself. Photos that Paul must've taken the day they went to the Botanical Gardens were clipped to several of them. *Should I be flattered or frightened?* Uncertain what to do, she closed the pad.

After tossing the towel on top of her clothes in the tub, she stepped into the hall and pulled the door closed behind her. Paul met her at the bottom of the stairs, holding a tray with a teapot and matching cups. A lantern dangled from one hand.

"Where's Annie?" she asked, following him into the small, cozy room she'd discovered the first time Amy had brought her for a latte.

"I dried her off with an old towel and showed her a comfy spot by the fire," Paul said, glancing toward the fireplace. "She lay down and went right to sleep."

"Thank you," Beth said, sitting on the edge of the loveseat cushion. She ran her fingers through her hair, trying to smooth it out.

Paul deposited the tray on the small, mahogany coffee table and placed the lantern on the floor next to it. "Here, this will warm you up," he said, pouring a cup of tea and handing it to her.

She took a cautious taste. "Mmm, peppermint. One of my favorites."

"Mine too." Paul said, sitting down next to her.

As Beth sipped her tea, she wondered what in the world had made Paul so angry. She speculated it had something to do with the storm but wasn't sure. "So? What do you have to say about scaring me like that?" she asked, sliding back onto the small couch.

Paul stared into the yellow orangish flames in the fireplace. "Alan Blake was my best friend," he began. "We were like brothers. We even decided to go to the same college after high school. The first semester of our freshman year, we came home for Thanksgiving. That weekend a terrific storm blew in, and we went out on the headland to watch the waves, just like you. It went against everything we'd been taught about storms and the ocean, but we were at that age when we knew it all and nothing could happen to us." He took another sip of his tea and set his cup down on the coffee table. "Anyway, we'd been out there for over an hour and had our backs turned to the ocean." He shook his head. "I don't even remember what had attracted our attention, but we weren't watching the waves like we should have been. Suddenly a gigantic wave struck us from behind and we were knocked off our feet. I managed to grab onto something, but Alan wasn't that lucky. The wave took him right off the ledge and down into the rocks. I tried to get to him, but he kept getting pulled further and further out. By the time I got back with help, he'd disappeared. They found his body the next day on a little beach to the south." Paul stopped and looked into Beth's eyes so intently she felt uncomfortable. "So when Amy told me you were out there in this storm, I panicked."

"But why were you were so angry?" she asked.

"I guess I was angry with myself because I couldn't save Alan, and I didn't want the same thing to happen to you." He reached over and placed his hand on her wrist. "Will you forgive me?"

Beth stared into her teacup. She didn't know how to respond; the man had frightened her badly. Finally, she offered him a slight smile and nodded.

Paul sighed as he leaned back, laced his fingers behind his head, and stretched his long legs out in front of him. "Are you hungry? Do you want something to eat?"

"Yes, I am, but how can we cook? The power is still out."

"The same way I heated the water. Remember the trash burner next to the stove in the kitchen? I'll just warm up some soup on it. Nothing fancy but it'll fill the void."

"What about your other guests?"

"Don't have any. No one is due until day after tomorrow, so we have the whole place to ourselves."

"And Clara?"

"It's her day off. I'm sure she's curled up in front of the fireplace in her bungalow — kind of like old Annie over there." He nodded toward the sleeping dog. "Now, how about that soup?" Paul stood, grabbed the lantern, and started toward the kitchen.

"What can I do to help?" Beth asked, setting down her cup and following him.

"Well, you can put together a couple of sandwiches. And I think there are some sodas in the fridge."

After a simple dinner of tomato soup and ham sandwiches, Beth curled up on the loveseat and watched Paul add logs to the fire. The storm had subsided, but the power had not come back on yet. Completely dark outside, the growing blaze bathed the sitting room in a warm glow.

Annie, who had enjoyed a couple of sandwiches herself, was stretched out on her side in front of the fire again and fast asleep.

"You might as well spend the night," Paul suggested, as he sat on his haunches and watched the flames. "It doesn't look like the power will be coming on any time soon and there is no sense freezing at your place. You can have the room next to mine."

"Thanks. I don't really want to walk home in the dark and then try to stay warm."

"Come on, and I'll get you settled." Paul grabbed the lantern as he got to his feet, and Beth followed him back up the stairs. Turning left again, he opened the other door at the end of the short hallway.

"Leave your door open and the heat will find its way in. I'll bring you something to help keep you warm." Paul walked out of the bedroom, leaving Beth in the dark. She slowly inched toward the bed, careful not to fall over any furniture. She had just reached it when he returned holding a lit oil lamp and one of the quilts she'd seen in the trunk at the foot of his bed.

"Did Annie come upstairs with us?"

"I don't think so." Paul set the lamp down on the small table next to the bed and stepped back into the hallway. "Annie, come on girl." A moment later, he returned to the room. "I didn't hear any movement down there."

"I don't think we're going to get her away from that fire," Beth said. "She hasn't had the opportunity to lie in front of one for quite awhile."

"Well, if you don't need anything else I shall bid you good night." With that, he handed over the quilt and walked out.

Beth shook out the handmade counterpane and let it float down over the bed. Then she turned back the covers. Slipping out of everything but her panties and T-shirt, she crawled in between the sheets. It wasn't long until the bed felt cozy and warm. As she dropped off to sleep, a jumble of thoughts passed through her head. She'd appreciated the space Paul had given her after the incident at the Botanical Gardens, but as she lay in the darkness she couldn't help but wonder what it would be like to lay next to him in that big brass bed, listening to his breathing and smelling the faint musky scent she'd begun to associate with him.

CHAPTER *18*

B eth Braddock opened the front door of the Mendocino Bed & Breakfast and was greeted by the pungent smell of giblets cooking on the stove. Leaving her constant canine companion by the fireplace in the quaint sitting room, she strolled through the dining room and into the rustic kitchen. There she found Paul standing at the stainless worktable and wrestling an enormous turkey into a roasting pan. Underneath his white chef's apron, he was casually dressed in grey sweats and a black muscleman shirt.

"Good morning," Beth said, placing a bag of groceries on the counter.

"You're here early," he grunted as he made a final adjustment of the large bird.

"I decided it would be easier to make the dressing here," she said, slipping off her denim jacket and hanging it on the hook on the back of the swinging door.

"I'm so glad you did. Definitely going to need help getting this thing in the oven." He patted the turkey a couple of times. "I 'bout got a hernia hauling it out of the cool room."

"Is it going to fit?" Beth asked, looking from the roasting pan to open door of the old, restaurant-style oven.

"Yeah, just barely. I measured and there should be a couple of inches to spare," Paul said, wiping his hands on the front of his apron.

"Where's Clara? I thought she'd be in charge of this venture."

"Remember I told you that she and my secretary were childhood chums?"

"Yes."

"Well, Gladys invited her to spend Thanksgiving with her and, because Clara hadn't had a vacation since before Mom got sick, I insisted that she go."

"You insisted? With Clara?"

Paul grinned. "Okay, so I kinda badgered her until she gave in. Now, let's mix up your dressing and stuff this thing."

"I think I have everything I need." She unpacked two yellow onions, a package of sausage, a large container of bread cubes, and small jars filled with sage and bay-leaf. "I wrote down Dad's recipe last night, best as I could remember." She pulled a folded piece of paper out of her hip pocket. "I just hope it turns out."

"Stop worrying, I'm sure it'll be fine. The giblets are done, so I'll chop them and brown the sausage while you get the other part started," he said, picking up the small white package. "You'll find measuring cups, spoons and a large stainless steel bowl on the counter. Let me know if you need anything else."

Beth read through the recipe, dumping ingredients into the bowl as she went. "Okay," she said a few minutes later, "I'm ready for the last two ingredients."

"Coming right up." Paul brought the aromatic meats over and dumped them into the mixture. Standing so close, she could feel the heat from his body and again imagined what it would be like to lie next to him, his arms wrapped around her. He picked up a large spoon and offered it to her. "Do you want to do the honors or shall I?"

"Oh, you go ahead. Are there hooks and twine to tie it shut?"

"Yeah, over on top of the stove." He turned and pointed with the spoon he'd been stirring with, flicking bits of dressing all over. Grabbing one of the legs, he said, "Okay you turkey, open up." Then he packed both ends of the large bird with the gooey dressing, and Beth helped him tie it shut. "Now, let's get him in the oven," he said, giving the turkey another playful pat.

As they grabbed the handles and lifted the roaster, the turkey shifted, and the pan tilted to one side. "Oh my, it's heavier than it looks," Beth said, straining to keep it level.

"Told you." Slowly, Paul began to back toward the oven.

Focused on the roasting pan, neither of them noticed Annie entering the kitchen. "Oh, look out!" Beth warned, but it was too late. Paul tumbled over the old dog and, without a free hand to catch himself, went crashing to the floor, pulling Beth along with him. She landed next to him, her head on his shoulder.

"Oh, are you all right?" she asked, getting to her knees and trying not to laugh. "You aren't hurt are you?"

"Only my dignity," he said, lying flat on his back. Free of its pan, the turkey had landed on his chest and was oozing dressing all over him.

Completely oblivious to the disaster she had created, Annie struggled to her feet and meandered out of the room. Beth and Paul looked at each other and burst out laughing.

"Now what?" she asked when she could finally speak.

"Well, fortunately the bird ended up on me so I think we can salvage it." He slid it off his chest and back into the roaster. Then he got to his feet and helped Beth up. "Let's have a look at it."

Together they lifted the huge pan, turkey and all, onto the stainless worktable. After a quick inspection and some minor adjustments, they started toward the oven again. This time Paul made sure there were no obstacles, namely a chocolate lab, in his way. With the turkey safely in the oven, they placed the remaining dressing into a casserole and crammed it into the fridge.

"I think we're set for now. About an hour before Tom and Amy are supposed to get here, I'll throw the dressing in the oven, whip up the mashed potatoes and make the gravy. Now, I guess I'd better get this mess cleaned up," Paul said, stripping off his dressing-soaked apron.

Beth looked at the mountain of dishes in the sink and the counters covered with clumps of food and immediately was reminded of the first time she'd helped out at the bed & breakfast. "I'll help you before I go."

"Great, and if you're not in a hurry, we can have lattes by the fire. I found a new flavor of syrup last week that I think you'll like."

After the kitchen was back to the cook's standard of cleanliness, the two of them moved into the sitting room where Annie, unaffected by the excitement earlier, was asleep in her favorite spot by the fire. Beth slipped off her shoes and curled up in one corner of the small couch. Paul sat on the floor in front her, reclining against it and stretching out his long legs.

"Mmm, this is really good," she said, after sampling her drink. "What is it?"

"Hot buttered rum. I had it at the coffee house in Fort Bragg and convinced the girl behind the counter to sell me a bottle."

Leaning around to place her mug on the coffee table, Beth found Paul's scent, a mixture of sweat and sports deodorant, slightly arousing. When he reached out his hand and slowly traced his fingers along the underside of her arm, chills went up her spine.

"I'm glad you're here," he said.

"Me too," she whispered, staring into his jade-colored eyes.

He reached up and gently caressed her hair. Slowly, he pulled her toward him, and this time she didn't resist. When their lips met, she felt a tingling sensation, and she was sure her heart skipped a beat.

Amy Thompson marveled at the feast before her; a plump, juicy turkey baked to a golden brown, the mountain of mashed potatoes next to a gallon of gravy, a heaping bowl of steaming dressing, creamy green bean casserole topped with crunchy onion bits, and dark red cranberry sauce. Glad she'd decided on braised Brussels sprouts and ambrosia salad, they balanced out the meal perfectly. Even Tom had brought a gigantic pumpkin pie he'd baked himself. And wine, of course.

Watching Paul carve the turkey, Amy thought about the first one she'd tried to cook while she was married to Rick. When it came out of the oven, it was almost black on the outside and raw on the inside. Never allowed in her mother's kitchen, she barely knew how to boil water, so how was she supposed to know it needed to be thawed first? Later, as Rick began clawing his way up the corporate ladder, he'd dragged her to social sideshows rather than have a proper Thanksgiving. By the time she'd divorced him, the holiday no longer meant that much, and that's why Paul's invitation to spend Thanksgiving at the bed & breakfast was too good to pass up.

"I would like to propose a toast," Tom said, lifting his wine glass. "Here's to good friends, good food, and good times."

Amy shook her head. "You sound like a beer commercial," she said, clinking her glass against his.

"I was thinking more along the lines of a fine wine," he retorted.

Of course you were.

"I've got one," Paul offered. "Here's to sudden snowstorms in the High Sierras."

"Huh?" Amy lowered her glass. "What do snowstorms have to do with fine wine?"

"Why do you think we have the place to ourselves? My two bookings for this holiday cancelled on account of the big storm. Great for privacy but bad for business."

"Oh," she said, nodding her head. "I get it."

Tom paused, his fork halfway to his mouth. "Does this mean we'll be getting stuck with a check at the end of the meal?"

"You better believe it. And for you, I'm charging double."

Amy chuckled. She loved the way the two men bantered back and forth, except when it came to politics; then it got ugly. Tom, a staunch Republican, was totally involved in what was happening politically. Paul, an Independent, could care less. Once, when the topic of war came up, Amy thought it was going to come to blows, but most of time it was just in fun.

"Now it's my turn." Beth raised her glass to eye level. "Like all of you, I came to Mendocino to start over. I found friends who had patience and understanding, a willingness to reach out, and..." She smiled at Paul. "You made me laugh again. Thanks for being my friends."

"Here, here," Amy said, holding her own glass high overhead.

"Tell me," Tom said in between bites, "how big is this old turkey bird?"

"Thirty pounds," Paul announced.

"Bet that was a bitch to stuff and get into the oven," Tom said, shaking his head.

"Naa." Paul winked at Beth. "Piece of cake."

Amy wouldn't swear to it, but she was almost certain Beth giggled. "Thirty pounds?" she asked, helping herself to another slice. "How hungry did you think we were going to be?"

"Originally there were going to be more people for dinner, remember? Looks like I'll be serving turkey sandwiches for days."

"Well, if you're handing out doggie bags, sign me up for one." Tom said, reaching out with his fork and spearing another serving of dark meat.

"Maybe I'll just freeze it and serve it again at Christmas," Paul suggested.

"That reminds me," Beth said. "I talked to Tony earlier, and he told me that he and Steve will be traveling this Christmas."

"Oh, really?" Amy piled more mashed potatoes on her plate and drowned them with gravy. "Where are they going?" As she waited for an answer, she put together the perfect bite of potatoes, gravy, turkey, dressing, and cranberry sauce. Placing it in her mouth, she savored the mingling of flavors.

"Oh, they thought they might go to the northern coast of California."

"Here?" Amy almost choked. "They're coming here?" she said around the enormous mouthful of food. Beth nodded. "I can hardly wait to meet them. I feel like I already know them." It was true. Beth's brother-in-law was a topic she spoke about often.

"And," Beth turned to Paul, "they'd like to stay here if you have a room available."

"No problem. I only have a couple of reservations so far. I'll put them down right now before I forget." He got up and left the room.

"So what made them decide to spend Christmas here?" Tom asked.

"Well, I've told them so much about you that they want to come down and meet you."

Amy leaned closer to Beth. "Does this mean things are getting serious?" she asked, hoping to find out just what was going on between her and Paul.

"Who's getting serious about what?" Paul asked as he came back into the dining room.

As a look of panic crossed Beth's face, Amy glanced at Tom but no help there. He just gave her the same look of amusement he always did when her mouth got her into trouble.

"Well..." Amy began.

"Believe me Paul," Tom said. "You don't want to know."

"If you say so." He turned to Beth. "They're all set. How long do you think they're going to stay?"

"Probably about a week. Both of them are pretty busy, and I doubt they can get away for longer than that."

"Well, I think we all should go to San Francisco while they're here." Amy hoped to keep the conversation moving along. "The stores are always so beautifully decorated. We might even go see a show."

"Excellent idea." Tom refilled his wine glass. "I'll check out what's going on and see about getting tickets. And since we're on the topic of shows, Amy was telling me about your pictures of the storm, Beth. She says they are really spectacular."

"Oh, they really are," Amy said. "Have you seen them, Paul?"

"No, as a matter of fact," he said, staring at his wine as he swirled it in his glass, "I haven't."

"Oh you really should. The way Beth captured the brutal force of the waves is breathtaking and..." Amy stopped short when she realized Paul was glaring at her. *Oh damn!* She'd forgotten how angry he'd been with Beth the day she took those pictures, risking her life during that horrible storm. "Um...anyway," she continued, trying to ignore Paul, "the pictures you took of the flowers are gorgeous. The roses look almost three-dimensional. And the rhododendrons, the reds and pinks..."

"So, when are you going to put together a showing?" Tom interrupted.

Amy sighed. *Thank you! I never know when to shut up!*

"Me? A show? I don't think that's a good idea." Beth shook her head. "They're not that good. After all, this is only a hobby."

"Why not?" Amy asked. "Suzy can help you get them mounted and up for display. You might even sell some of them."

"She's right," Paul added. "Photos as great as yours should be on display."

Amy was almost certain that with a little more coaxing, Beth just might agree to do it.

"Well, thank you for being so supportive and for making my first Thanksgiving without..." Beth's voice caught, and she took a sip of water before continuing. "I wouldn't have been able to bear it without you."

CHAPTER 19

Beth Braddock stood on her front porch while the light rain dwindled to a drizzle, watching Annie sniff around the yard and listening to the bong of a distant buoy. *Where can they be?* "I hope Tony's Porsche didn't have trouble navigating the storm," she told the big dog.

As she turned to go inside in search of a jacket, a gunmetal-grey Humvee pulled up. Accustomed to having strange cars park in front of her house six months of the year, she ignored it. Annie, however, did not. Leaving her explorations, she started jumping up and down at the front gate. Looking again, Beth recognized the occupants of the large vehicle and dashed down the sidewalk.

"Where did this come from?" she demanded, opening the front gate.

"Don't look at me," Steve said, stepping out and stretching his legs. "It's Tony's. He thinks he's Horatio from *CSI: Miami.*"

"Oh, really?" Beth embraced the sandy-haired man. "I always thought of him as a Gil Grissom. You know, the quiet brainy type."

"Knock it off, you two," Tony said, coming around the large vehicle. Annie jumped up and planted her paws in the middle of his chest. "Why hello, Annie, how are you?" He gave her ears a vigorous scratching.

"Get down, Girl." Beth scolded. "Down."

"And how's my favorite sister-in-law?" He wrapped his arms around Beth's waist and lifted her off the ground.

"I'm your only sister-in-law," she said, returning the hug. "I'm terrific and so glad you're here."

"Let me look at you." Tony put her down and stepped back. Beth held out her arms and spun around. "You look absolutely radiant. Must be the ocean air."

She smiled. *Among other things.* "I can hardly wait for you to meet my friends. Paul has made dinner arrangements for all of us at a restaurant in Noyo Harbor. I hope that's okay."

"Sounds great, but first I want to get out of these clothes," Steve said, looking down at his wrinkled Dockers. "I feel like I've had them on for days. Where's this bed & breakfast we're supposed to be staying at anyway?"

"It's a block off Main Street. Give me a second to lock the house and chain up Annie, and I'll show you where it is," Beth said.

"Do you have to chain the old girl up?" Tony asked, patting the chocolate lab on the head.

"If I don't, she jumps the fence. I don't want her to get hit."

"Well then, bring her along," Tony said. "There's plenty of room."

Leaving the dog where she was, Beth hurried back into the house, grabbed her keys, and locked the door on her way out. When she returned to the Humvee, Steve was holding the front passenger door open for her. "You sit here, and I'll jump in the back with Annie," he said.

"Always the gentleman," Beth said, planting a brief kiss on his cheek. She climbed in and settled back into the civilian version of the military vehicle. "Wow, there is a lot of room in here. Maybe you should be our driver tonight.

That is, if you're not too tired. It'll be nicer than taking separate vehicles."

"Sure. After a hot shower, I'll be as good as new," Tony said, starting up the Humvee.

Steve sighed from the back. "If only it were that simple." Tony glared at him in the rearview mirror as he pulled away from the curb, and Beth giggled at their playful banter.

"Checkout that wicked-looking tree," Tony said, pulling up in front of the Mendocino Bed & Breakfast. "What kind is it?"

"It's a holly tree," Beth said as they climbed out. "In the spring, it puts on beautiful white blossoms." She waited in front of the gate as the two men grabbed their luggage. "Paul's great-aunt planted it when she bought this place. It's supposed to ward off evil."

"Looks to me like it's trying to take over the entire yard," Steve said, coming up behind her, a suitcase in each hand.

"Paul's been threatening to cut it back, but I don't think he's touched it."

"Why? Is he superstitious?" Tony asked, joining them.

Beth laughed. "I don't know. You'll have to ask him." Leaving Annie to nose around the yard, she led the way through the gate and up the narrow sidewalk. After opening the door, they squeezed into the small lobby where her photograph of the bed & breakfast hung in a place of honor. The faint clinking of dishes was a clear indication that preparations for the evening meal were under way, and the aroma of roasting meat drifted from the kitchen.

"What smells so good?" Steve asked, setting the bags on the floor in front of the carved wooden counter.

Beth inhaled deeply. "Smells like Clara's pork loin.

She rubs it with rosemary and bakes it until the outside is crispy. It's very delicious."

Steven's stomach growled loudly. "Are you sure we have to eat out?" he asked, placing his hand over it.

"Wait here, and I'll go get Paul." Beth started toward the dining room but came to an abrupt halt as the owner burst through the doorway, drying his hands with a towel. Strands of his dark wavy hair hung down in his eyes and small beads of perspiration had formed along his hairline. Dressed in loose-fitting faded denims and a black T-shirt that accentuated his muscular arms, Beth smiled as she caught Steve giving him the once-over. Playfully nudging him in the ribs, she whispered, "Back off, he's mine," and then giggled when he glared at her.

"You must be Paul." Beth's brother-in-law extended his right hand. "I'm Tony Braddock and this is my friend, Steve Lawson." The men exchanged handshakes.

"It's so good to finally meet you. I feel like I already know you." Paul smiled and glanced at Beth, and then he looked at her again. She returned the smile, enjoying the effect she seemed to be having on the man.

"Likewise. Beth has kept us so well-informed about her new friends, we had to come down here and meet you for ourselves."

"Uh...well, let's get you checked in," Paul said, moving around behind the counter. He kept glancing at Beth, his eyebrows knitting ever so slightly as he did. "Has Beth talked to you about dinner?" he asked when the formality of the paperwork had been completed.

"Yes, and it sounds great. We'd just like to shower and shave first."

"No problem. That'll give me time to make sure the dining room is set up for Clara to serve dinner and then change my own clothes."

"And you haven't heard the best part, Paul." Beth slid up to the counter. "Tony's going to take all of us in his car."

"All of us?" Paul frowned again. "I thought you told me he drove a Porsche."

"He did, but he's got a new ride. Wait until you see it."

Amy Thompson took one last look at her reflection in the mirror before going downstairs to wait for Tom. Her hair, a mass of loose curls that hung to her shoulders, was swept up softly at the sides and secured with rhine-stone clips. *Not bad — should get somebody's attention.* She draped her lacy, black shawl on the chair by the front door, went into the kitchen and poured herself a glass of wine. Returning to the living room, she sat on the couch and thought about Beth and Paul. Some kind of relation-ship was developing, she was sure of it. The signs were all there, stolen looks at one another and the almost constant smiles on their faces.

She had just drained her wine glass when she heard Tom's little Z3 pull into the driveway. As she opened the front door, Tom walked in, dressed in his grey flannel pants and navy sports jacket. "Well, don't you look hand-some tonight," Amy said as she closed the door.

"What? This?" He glanced down as if he'd forgotten what he had on. "Yeah thanks," he said, heading for the kitchen.

Following him, Amy frowned as she looked down at her long-sleeve velvet dress. Clinging to her frame in a most flattering way, it stopped just above her strappy high heels, and its sapphire color intensified her blue eyes. *Ap-parently, my choice of attire is wasted on you!*

"Would you like some wine?" she asked, setting down

her wine glass and retrieving a second one from the cupboard.

"I thought you'd never ask," he said. She poured some in his glass and handed it over. Tom passed it under his nose a couple of times before sipping it. "Hmmm, this is a nice little cabernet. Where did you get it?" He asked, picking up the bottle and inspecting the label.

Amy waited until he took another sip. "At the outlet store." She held her breath and waited. Tom's face lost all expression, and he looked like he was about to gag. "This is two buck chuck?" he asked after forcing himself to swallow. Giggling, Amy nodded. He swirled the dark red liquid in his glass and cautiously took another sip. "You know, it's really not bad."

"Yeah, I thought it was pretty good too," Amy said, refilling her own glass. She stepped around the island, opened the French doors, and moved out onto the deck. Tom trailed along behind her and the two of them stood silently, watching the waves move into the small bay.

"So, were you able to come up with something for Beth to wear tonight?" Tom asked a few minutes later.

Amy nodded. "I think you'll be pleasantly surprised. It is quite a change from..." A low rumble interrupted her and rattled the windows. "What the heck is that?" She moved back toward the living room, setting her wine glass on the counter as she passed through the kitchen.

"Sounds like a large vehicle of some kind," Tom said, stopping long enough to refill his glass.

Headlights flooded the house with bright light, and just as Amy reached out, a loud knocking shook the door.

"We're here," Beth announced as she and Paul burst into the room, with two other men in tow. The borrowed outfit looked better than Amy had imagined. The straight leg of the dark green pants and the black patent-leather heels made her legs look much longer. The plunging neckline of the white blouse gave the black jacket a more feminine look, and her crystal earrings accentuated the jacket's metallic stitching. "Amy and Tom, this is my brother-in-law, Tony, and his friend, Steve."

"Finally, a face to put with the name," Amy said, hugging both of them. "Welcome to Mendocino."

"Glad to meet you," Tom said, moving forward and shaking hands.

"Do we have time for a drink?" Amy asked.

"Well, our reservation is for seven," Paul said, checking his watch, "so we probably should get going. We can get a drink in the bar, and there's always a chance that we might get a table early."

"Sounds good. Tom and I can follow you," Amy said, reaching for her shawl.

"Well, —" Paul stopped. "Here, let me help you with that." He took her shawl and gently wrapped it around her shoulders. "You look amazing in that dress."

"Why thank you," Amy said, planting a small kiss on his cheek. *Glad someone noticed!*

"Uh, you were saying," Tom prodded.

"What? Oh yeah. We can all go in Tony's rig, if you like," Paul suggested.

"The Porsche?" Tom asked.

Steve turned to Beth. "Is there anything you haven't told these people?"

"I haven't shared everything —" She grinned at him. "— yet!"

"I bought a Humvee," Tony explained. "And Beth has volunteered me to drive tonight."

"A Hummer?" Tom's eyes widened. "I've always wanted to check out one of those."

"Well, sounds like it's your lucky night," Amy grumbled,

whisking his wine glass away and taking it to the kitchen. *Wish it could be mine.*

By the time she returned to the living room, everyone had moved out onto the porch. She turned off the lights and grabbed her clutch bag as she went out the front door, locking it behind her.

"Wait 'til you see the inside of this thing," Beth whispered as she moved closer to Amy. "A person could live inside of it, I think."

"Looks like Tom can hardly contain himself," Amy said, nodding toward the large vehicle. Paul, Tony and Steve were standing at the end of the sidewalk chatting, while Tom circled the rig, peeking in each window as he went by.

As the two women approached, Steve stepped forward and opened the front passenger door. "You can ride in front," he said, smiling at Amy.

Tom had just rounded the back right fender and proceeded to slide into the offered seat. "Great! I've always wanted to check out the instrument panel in one of these. I've heard it looks like an airplane cockpit."

"Looks like you're in the last seat with me," Steve said to Amy as he slammed the vehicle door.

"That suits me just fine," Amy said, crossing her arms.

Paul and Beth were still standing off to the side, so Steve opened the back door, deftly disengaged the seat, and held his hand out for Amy. As soon as the two of them where settled, Paul righted the seat, and he and Beth piled in.

Tony fired up the engine, and Amy was almost certain Tom let out a small squeal. *This evening is definitely going to be interesting, to say the least.* As the massive vehicle backed out of the driveway and headed toward Highway 1, her own pulse quickened as she experienced its sheer power, so unlike her own Volkswagen Beetle. As the Humvee cruised toward Fort Bragg, she couldn't help but notice Paul and Beth, their heads pressed together and whispering to each other. And even though the interior of the vehicle was dark, she would've sworn they'd kissed. *Definitely gonna quiz Beth about that later.* She could hear Tom babbling in the front seat as he checked out all the gadgets and compartments he could find, asking Tony all sorts of questions. By the time they pulled down into the wharf, Amy was ready to bail.

The restaurant, illuminated by recessed lighting and candles on the tables, was dark and inviting. *Very romantic!* Gold stars and tinsel hung from the ceiling and a large Christmas tree stood at the end of the bar. Paul sent the group into the lounge while he checked in with the hostess. Tony bought the first round of drinks and then went back to join him.

Amy settled into a large cushioned barstool and looked around. Tom was having a discussion with the bartender about the finer points of a good wine. Beth, who was seated on the other side of her, was sharing a quiet conversation with Steve. Amy turned her chair until she could see Paul and Tony. They were talking and, every now and then, one of them would look in Beth's direction. Their discussion seemed intense but not hostile. *What on earth can they be talking about?* Finally they joined the others at the bar.

"It should only be a few more minutes," Paul said, standing behind Beth.

"Good," Amy said, "I'm starving."

After a few minutes of simultaneous conversations, the six of them were seated at a table overlooking the Noyo Harbor. As they watched the last of the fishing boats chug by, their running lights reflected in the water, a mammoth of a man wearing an immense black apron approached the table. "Good evening," he said in a robust baritone voice. "I'm Angelo, and I'll be your waiter. Does anyone need a refill on drinks or would you like to start with an appetizer?"

"I'll have another cabernet," Tom said, setting his empty glass on the table. "No, wait. Better yet, bring us two bottles of Arger-Martucci Syrah. My treat."

"Very well. Anyone else?" Angelo asked. The others shook their heads.

"You're going to love this wine," Tom said. "It won a silver medal at The San Francisco Chronicle Wine Competition."

Angelo came right back, and Amy wanted to hide when Tom made a big deal about sniffing the cork and tasting the wine before allowing it to be served. *Such a pompous ass sometimes.*

After the waiter had taken everyone's order and disappeared toward the kitchen, Steve remarked, "That is one big dude!"

"Yeah, he kind of looks like a long-haired Hoss Cartwright," Beth said.

"With a name like Angelo, I wonder if he moonlights for the Godfather." Tony offered.

"Oh, no Godfather jokes." Beth held up both hands.

"What's wrong with *The Godfather*?" Paul asked. "It's a classic."

"Not you too," she moaned. "Tony and Craig both worked in the movie theater the summer it hosted a *The Godfather* festival. They watched all three movies so much they could say the dialogue along with the actors. It became such an obsession with them that everything was connected to it somehow." Beth looked at Tony and let out a large sigh. "I had forgotten how annoying it was." He shrugged his shoulders and smiled.

"I need to use the ladies room before dinner." Amy turned to Beth. "Why don't you come with me?"

"Oh, I don't..." Amy gave her a quick kick with her foot. "Uh, yeah sure," Beth said, frowning as she got to her feet. "We'll be right back."

Amy practically pulled Beth to the restrooms. As soon as they were inside, she started in. "First — are you all right?"

"You mean the sigh? Oh, yeah. Just one of those memories that sneak up on you, but I'm fine." Beth looked at herself in the mirror over the sink. "I'm still getting used to these highlights. I look so different."

Amy stood next to her and looked into the eyes of Beth's reflection. "So how did Paul like your new look and your outfit?"

Beth laughed. "When I took Tony and Steve to the bed & breakfast, he did a double take when he saw me and seemed terribly distracted. It was all I could do to keep from laughing."

"Oh that's too perfect. Okay last question." Amy tugged at Beth's arm, forcing her to turn and face her. "What the hell is going on?"

"What are you talking about?"

"I saw the two of you kissing on the way here."

"Oh, that." Beth waved her off.

"Yes, that. Are you two getting serious?"

"What would you call getting serious?"

"Beth!"

"Okay, okay. Our relationship is growing but I wouldn't call it serious," Beth said, avoiding Amy's persistent gaze by looking at herself again in the mirror.

Amy continued to stare at Beth's profile for several seconds. "Well, we should probably go back before they get suspicious."

"I thought you had to go."

"Not really, I just wanted to talk to you privately," she said, pulling the door open.

As they made their way through the restaurant, Amy felt a twinge of jealousy. *Why?* Maybe it was because Paul was so kind to Beth, and they looked so cute together. It made Amy look at her own love life. *Do I even have one?* She couldn't remember the last time she'd walked with someone holding hands or shared long, intense kisses. She had been so ready to be rid of her ex-husband, Rick, the possibility of missing physical contact had never crossed her mind. But now, watching Beth and Paul, she realized it was a void that needed to be filled. She thought about Tom. In fact, she had been thinking about him a lot lately. *Could our friendship turn into something more?*

Amy, who was a few feet ahead of Beth, noticed that Tom and Steve were involved in a heated discussion, while Tony and Paul were having a quiet conversation of their own. As she approached the table she heard Paul say, "I find myself really caring about Beth. If fact, I think I..." He stopped when he saw Amy. Tom and Steve, however, seemed to be oblivious to everything else around them.

"What in the world are you two talking about, Tom?" Beth asked, taking her seat between him and Paul.

"I had merely asked Steve here what his stance was on same sex marriage," Tom explained.

"You what?" Amy's eyes moved from Tom to Steve. The look on Steve's face plainly showed his annoyance.

"I asked Steve..." Tom began.

"Never mind, I heard you!" Amy interrupted. She couldn't believe how tactless Tom could be.

"And I was telling him," Steve said, in what Amy believed was his best lawyer voice, "that while some couples we know have experienced that bonding, it's not something Tony and I feel is necessary for our relationship. We have legal documents in place in case something happens to one of us, but right now..."

"Yes, but do you think it's a good idea to have it legalized? I mean think of what it could do to..."

"Tom!" Amy hissed. "That's enough! Change the subject." Her china-blue eyes launched daggers at him.

"Okay, okay. Don't have a hemorrhage." Tom took a big sip of his wine.

Amy looked up just in time to see Angelo coming toward the table, a huge tray balanced between his shoulder and his outstretched arm. She was never so glad to see anyone. Tom would have a more difficult time sticking his foot in his mouth if it was full of food.

CHAPTER 20

Tom Miller had just finished with his last customer and locked up when the big, brown UPS van lurched to a stop in front of the bookstore. "Hey Jake," Tom said as the driver bounded down the van's steps. "How's it going?"

"Oh man, I got so many deliveries left to make it'll be midnight before I'm done."

"On Christmas Eve?"

"Oh yeah. This is our busiest day of the year." He handed over the rectangular shaped package he'd been holding. "Seems like everyone waits 'til the last minute anymore." Then he turned on his heel and climbed back into the delivery van, taking the steps two at a time.

"Well thanks," Tom called, waving the package at him, "and Merry Christmas."

Jake released the parking brake and dropped the transmission into drive. "Yeah man, back at ya," he said, raising one hand and roaring off down Main Street.

Tom checked his watch as he hurried up the stairs to his apartment. A few minutes past six — should have plenty of time to shower and change before heading to the bed & breakfast. Spending the first twenty years of his life celebrating Christmas with seven other siblings as well as both sets of grandparents, the last thing he wanted was a scripted gathering immersed in family tradition. He might share a meal or two with Amy but usually spent most of the holiday inventorying his books and wine, reordering his top sellers, discounting the surplus, and catching up on his reading. But this year promised to be something different, even though dinner the other night had started off badly. By the time they'd consumed the food and wine that had been ordered, there were no hard feelings, and everyone had a good time.

Placing the package on the counter, Tom selected the wines he planned to take and slipped them into his neoprene tote. Then he grabbed the scissors from his knife drawer, cut open the end of the package, and slid out some kind of bottle encased in bubble wrap. Unrolling it, he was intrigued to find a bottle of red wine with a plain white label adorned with a single yellow carnation and nothing else. He set it down on the counter and checked inside the empty box. Finding nothing, he flipped the box around and looked at the label. The return address had no name, only a post office box in Los Angeles that he didn't recognize.

"Wonder if this came from Two Buck Chuck," he muttered out loud. Charles Miller, who taught at the same school where Tom had been librarian and was no relation, shared Tom's love of great wines as well as his surname. They often tried to outdo one another by finding the "perfect" wine, but he hadn't heard from Chuck in years.

Tom stepped over to his computer and wiggled the mouse. When the web browser had loaded, he googled "yellow carnation wine," but nothing remotely related to wine came up. Completely baffled, he checked his watch again. *Better get moving or I'll be late.* Leaving everything on the counter for the time being, he headed for the bathroom.

Twenty minutes later, he emerged dressed in black slacks, a dark grey shirt and a light weight maroon sweater. Temporarily forgetting about the mysterious delivery, he gathered up the gifts he'd acquired — a gourmet cookbook for Amy, a bottle of the pinot noir from the Napa Valley for Paul, a season pass to the Botanical Garden for Beth, a pink plaid Snuggie for Clara, and a couple more bottles of wine from his collection for Tony and Steve — along with the neoprene tote, loaded them into his BMW Z3, and headed up Albion Street to the bed & breakfast.

Paul Hayden loaded the last few chunks of wood into the back of his Honda Element and headed back inside. On his way to the kitchen, he made a mental check of what they'd need; chairs, blankets, lighter fluid. As he watched Clara put the finishing touches on Margaret Hayden's famous hot cocoa, he felt like he was forgetting something but couldn't put his finger on what. "We about ready to go?" he asked.

"Fetch me that fancy drink dispenser off the top shelf of the pantry."

Paul smiled as he did as he was told. The double pump thermos, decorated with broad stripes of yellow, orange and red, had often accompanied the family trio on picnics, especially at the traditional New Year's bonfire. "Here you go," he said, setting it on the stainless steel worktable.

"Grab those blankets I stacked in the laundry room, while I fill this."

"I already packed some."

"Uh-huh." Clara did not continue as she carefully poured the hot drink into each chamber of the jug. "Which ones?" she asked when she was finally done.

"The old ones we used to have on the beds."

"Well, you go grab those heavier ones I set out." She

snapped shut the twin lids. "Don't want to be freezing my butt off tonight. It's supposed to be downright cold, the weatherman says."

"Yes ma'am, right away." Paul collected the blankets and took them to the car, where he inventoried what he'd packed one more time. *Still feel like I'm forgetting something.* He hustled back into the house and hauled out the huge basket of food that Clara had prepared. Just imagining what wonderful food she'd placed inside made his stomach growl. After sliding it into place in the back of the Honda, he slammed the hatch closed. "Did you put out the note and lock the door?" he asked Clara as she clumped down the sidewalk, clutching her wool coat closed and dangling her purse from her right elbow.

"Of course I did," she said, readjusting its short strap.

"Are you sure you want to lug that purse around? You won't need it on the beach."

"A lady does not go anywhere without her handbag. Now open that door of mine, so I can get in."

"Yes ma'am," Paul said, dashing around the vehicle and opening the door. As soon as Clara was settled, he climbed in behind the wheel and headed to Amy's house.

"I can't believe I've never done this on New Year's Eve," Amy said climbing into the backseat behind Paul after the two of them had loaded her stuff into the back. "I didn't even know people did this."

"It started a long time ago before this area turned into such a tourist attraction," Paul explained as he pulled away. "Folks who didn't have a lot of money would meet at Big River State Beach where they'd build a huge bonfire, share what food or drink they'd brought and celebrate the New Year. But as more and more people came here, it kinda got out of hand."

"And once Maggie got sick, God rest her soul, we didn't go anymore." Clara shook her head. "Just too hard on her."

They rode in silence the rest of the way to bookstore, where Tom was standing on the sidewalk, wrapped in the black and white fleece blanket he kept on the back of his couch and cradling some kind of long, narrow bag with built-in handles.

"What on earth is he holding?" Paul asked.

Amy leaned toward the middle and peered through the windshield. "That's his neoprene wine tote. He never goes anywhere without it. In fact, he brought it to your place the other night. Didn't you see it?"

"Nope, must have missed it," Paul said, bringing the car to a halt.

"Good evening, Miss Clara," Tom said as he piled into the backseat. "Paul, Amy. Looks like we lucked out on the weather, eh?" He set the tote between his feet and fastened his seatbelt. "I assume the others are meeting us there?"

"They're coming down from Bragg. Some errand Tony wanted to do with Beth before they leave tomorrow." Paul eased back onto Main Street and headed south on Highway 1. In less than a mile, he turned left onto North Big River Road and followed it down to the large beach.

"Tom, if you'll help me unload this wood, we can get the fire going while Amy and Clara start to set up camp."

"You got it." The men met at the back of the vehicle and had the wood unloaded and stacked by the fire pit in a few minutes.

While Tom helped unload the rest of the stuff, Paul doused the pieces of wood he'd arranged with the lighter fluid and then stopped. "Damn it, I knew I'd forgotten something."

"What's the problem?" Amy asked, setting down the armload of blankets she'd hauled over from the car. Tom was right behind her, lugging the picnic basket, and Clara brought up the rear, using the two chairs she was carrying like canes as she navigated across the sandy beach.

"I didn't grab anything to light the fire. I don't suppose you have a lighter or matches on you."

"Sorry, can't help you." Amy giggled as she spun on her heel and headed back for the last load.

"Tom, how about you? Got any kind of fire starter?"

The man set the basket down on a large flat rock. "Nope."

"Never fails." Clara shook her head. "Always seems like you forget one thing or t'other to start this here fire with." She stepped over to the picnic basket and opened it. "Looks like you remember this," she said, pulling out a smaller container of lighter fluid and setting it on the rock next to the basket, "so you must be needing this." She held out a long, red multipurpose lighter.

"Yes ma'am," Paul said, reaching out and taking it. "Thank you."

Clara smiled and winked at him. "Now get that fire going before we all freeze to death."

Paul beamed back at her. "Right away!"

While he got the blaze going, the other three spread blankets and set up chairs. They had just gathered around the fire pit when the gunmetal-grey Humvee coasted down the road and pulled in next to Paul's Honda Element.

"Hi guys," Beth called as she slid down out of the passenger seat.

Paul strolled over and gave her a hug. "Get everything taken care of?"

"Sure did. Look," she said, tugging something out of the right front pocket of her jeans. "I'm the proud owner of a new iPhone." She held out a cell phone in a floral case for all to see.

"An iPhone? But..." Paul stepped back. "One of the best buys on the market today is the Microsoft Phone. While it is a bit larger than the iPhone, it offers software more compatible to ..."

Clara cleared her throat from somewhere behind him; Paul stopped and looked around. Everyone was staring at him. "Uh, sorry." He chuckled. "After all those years at Microsoft, hard to break old habits, I guess." He turned back to Beth. "That's great that you have a cell phone."

"It was mostly for Tony." She smiled at her brother-in-law.

"That's right. Point your finger at me," Tony mock scolded her. "Just wanted a way to stay in touch more easily, now that you aren't sitting home alone."

"Well, I think it's a great idea." Amy stepped around the row of large boulders that served as a barrier between the road and the beach, and linked arms with Beth. "I have an iPhone too," she said, flashing Paul a smirk, "and I'd be happy to show you all its terrific features." Then the two of them led the way over to the fire pit.

As the rest of the group followed, Tom located his wine tote and removed the mystery bottle of wine that had arrived Christmas Eve along with his opener. "I brought this to celebrate. Looks like this is as good a time as any." He set it down and began his well-practiced method of uncorking.

"What, no commentary?" Amy asked. "No explanation of flavors or where the grapes were grown or what food it goes with?"

Tom shook his head. "Not this time because there's nothing to tell." He held up the bottle. "I have no idea what this is."

"Where did you get it?" Paul asked.

"It arrived via UPS. I think it came from an old colleague of mine, but I don't know for sure. Miss Clara, I assume you packed cups or glasses," he said, pulling the cork free.

"Yessir, right here in the basket." She ambled over next to him, pulled out a short tube of Styrofoam cups, and began handing them out. Tom followed along behind, pouring a small amount of the wine into each one until the bottle was empty. Raising his glass high he said, "Here's to..."

"Eww," Amy exclaimed, holding her cup away from her face. "This doesn't smell right. Did you smell this?" she asked Tom.

"Well, no – not yet." He lowered his cup, waved it in front of his nose and inhaled deeply. "It does have an odd bouquet."

Amy sniffed her own cup again. "You know, I happened to knock a bottle of those Black Sapphire products off the shelf and broke it a couple of days ago. It kinda had the same pungent odor."

The others cautiously sniffed the contents of their own cups.

"Cloves," Clara said.

"Who puts cloves in wine?" Tony asked.

"Maybe it's mulled wine," Tom suggested, looking at the label again. "But there's no way of knowing."

"What was in the bottle that broke?" Beth asked Amy.

"One of those silly love potions Sandy had convinced me to carry. I'll be so glad when they are all gone," she said, tossing her wine into the fire. As it hit the blaze, a burst of pink flame flashed, and then disappeared.

"What the hell was that?" Steve gazed into his own cup.

"No idea," Tom said, slowly shaking his head. "But I think we better..."

"Absolutely!" Paul agreed, and without any hesitation, the group tossed the rest of the suspect liquid into the fire, creating a spontaneous, burning bouquet of pink flames.

"Well, now that that's taken care of," Clara said, pulling the double pump thermos closer, "who wants some hot cocoa?"

"Me!" the group cried in unison, converging on the short, white-haired woman. After rinsing out their cups with a bottle of water Clara retrieved from the enormous picnic basket, they formed a line like kids in a cafeteria and waited patiently for the chocolaty drink.

"Mmm, this is delicious," Amy said. "Why haven't I tried it before?"

"It's one of those 'special occasions only' things, like the maple nut scones," Paul said.

A huge smile spread across Tom's face, and his eyes kind of glazed over. "Mmmm, maple nut scones."

Steve leaned toward Tony. "I think we're missing something here."

"Well, you see..." Paul began.

"Ever since this fella was a youngster," Clara interrupted, nodding her head at him, "I've made him maple nut scones as a special treat for his birthday, which is probably a good thing because he practically eats the whole batch in one day."

"I do not!" Paul interjected. "I..."

"Oh, pshaw! You really think I don't see you stuffing yourself with them, one after another. Surprised you didn't make yourself sick. And apparently, now you've got a partner in crime."

"Guilty as charged," Tom said, offering her a sheepish grin.

"I knew it!" Steve pointed his index finger at Tom. "A

lawyer's nightmare." He looked so serious, everyone busted out laughing.

While the group regained their composure, Clara pulled a checkered tablecloth from the basket and spread it out on the rock. "If you boys are done with your shenanigans, we probably should get to eatin' before our supper gets cold."

"Here," Amy said, joining her at the large, flat rock, "let me help you."

As the two began pulling things out of the picnic basket, Paul stepped closer to Beth. "I'd like to show you something if you'll come with me for just a minute."

Beth glanced at Clara and Amy, who were removing thick towels from around a large pot and rectangular casserole. "I don't want to upset Clara if we keep her waiting," she whispered as she looked up into his eyes.

"We won't be gone long enough to do that, I promise."

Beth smiled. "Okay, what do you want to show me?"

He grabbed her hand and began leading her toward the trail that left the beach and headed to where Big River emptied into the Pacific Ocean.

"Mind you don't be gone too long, Paul Michael Hayden," Clara called after them.

He grinned at Beth. "Yes ma'am, we won't!" he called back.

When they returned to the fire several minutes later, everyone was enjoying the food Clara had prepared. Avoiding her reprimanding glare, Paul lifted the lid on the red enameled pot. "You're in for a treat," he told Beth, ladling the contents into a bowl and handing it to her. "This is her lentil stew made with spicy sausage. She usually serves it with cornbread." He lifted a corner of the foil covering the rectangular-shaped casserole. Large, yellow squares almost two inches high were piled underneath.

"Not sure what's under here." Checking the other end, Paul was suddenly transported back in time. "You made mac-a-muffins!" He turned to Beth. "I haven't had these since I was a kid." He served himself a heaping bowl of stew and piled on two of the muffins made of macaroni and cheese. Then he and Beth joined the others sitting around the campfire to enjoy the feast.

CHAPTER 21

Beth Braddock stood on the headland trail, looking toward where the sky met the water. The holidays were over; the past week had flown by. The six of them had a wonderful time getting to know each other, but now Tony and Steve were on their way home. In fact, it had only been a few hours ago that she and Tony had been standing on this very spot.

"Are you happy?" Tony had asked, placing his hands on her shoulders and gazing into her eyes.

"Yes I am."

"I gotta tell you I had my doubts when you first moved here. I only agreed to help you do this because it was very obvious you couldn't stay where you were. But here you are, looking great, doing something you enjoy, and spending time with friends who genuinely care about you. Although that one guy can be annoying at times."

Beth laughed. "That's our Tom."

"I want you to know that Paul and I have had several conversations over the past week."

Beth frowned at him.

"I needed to know for myself what his intentions were."

"Gee, Dad." She wrapped her arms around Tony.

"He really cares about you. Not just because he told me so, but because I've watched him when he's with you, the way he looks at you, touches you. Beth, I'm quite certain the man is in love with you."

Beth blushed as she thought about Paul's warm embrace and lingering kiss they'd shared when they wandered out onto the rocks at Big River. It seemed strange to have Craig's brother talking about someone else loving her.

"I suspected he might be," Beth said. "He's been so patient, giving me time to think things through for myself."

"How do you feel about him?"

"I look forward to our time together and feel comfortable when I'm around him." Beth loosed her grasp and stepped away from Tony, not sure if she should say more.

"And?"

Beth turned to look at the man who was so much like her husband. She wanted to tell him her feelings but was afraid it would hurt him. "What?"

"I've been watching you too, you know. You lean into him when you're close to each other. You watch him when he's talking, and reach out to hold his arm. I've even seen you checking out his..."

"All right, all right," Beth interrupted, holding up her hands. "Yes, I find him extremely attractive, and it seems to intensify each time I see him."

"That's what I'd call being in love, wouldn't you?"

"I suppose I feel something, but it's different from what I felt with Craig. I guess it could be love." Beth searched Tony's face, looking for any signs that what she'd said hurt him. But all she'd seen was a kind of relief.

Now, as Beth stood looking at the ocean, she wondered how she would feel the next time she saw Paul. Now that she knew he loved her, and that she had admitted to having some kind of feeling for him. *Will it make things more comfortable or more awkward?* "Come on Annie," she called to the chocolate lab who'd been nosing around the rocks below. "Let's go." She'd find out soon enough.

* * *

Beth snuggled into her favorite spot on the small couch in the cozy sitting room. Paul was in the kitchen preparing his version of his mother's world-famous hot cocoa. All the guests had checked out and Clara had returned to her little bungalow behind the bed & breakfast.

"Here we are," he said, setting a tray on the small coffee table. Annie raised her head, but finding nothing to interest her, lowered it back down and closed her eyes.

Paul handed Beth a delicate cup filled with the steaming cocoa. "These really are beautiful," Beth said, admiring the cup and matching saucer.

"They belonged to my great-great-grandmother. Apparently they were among the few items that survived the family's trip out west in a covered wagon. They were packed in the trunk that now sits at the foot of my bed."

Beth recalled that day in November when she'd been in Paul's bedroom. She hadn't been there since, even though the opportunity had presented itself more than once. Still she'd resisted, even after she knew how Paul felt.

"Beth? Where are you?"

She blinked and looked around. Paul was sitting beside her on the couch, watching her. "Oh, I'm sorry. I was thinking about your room?"

"Really?" A smile flashed across his face. "What about my bedroom?"

"I was just remembering how it looked and the old trunk you mentioned."

"Are you sure you're remembering it correctly? We

could go up and look at it again. Just to make sure you have it right."

Beth hesitated. Here was another opportunity. *Am I going to turn it down as well?* Paul, moved closer and placed his arm around her shoulders, and, with his other hand, took her cup and set it on the table. She didn't pull away but, instead, settled in next to him and placed her head on his chest. He hugged her and began to playing with her hair.

"I really like what you've done with this," he said running his fingers through it. He gently caressed the side of her face. Noticing how warm and smooth his hand felt, Beth looked up into his eyes. Paul leaned down and pressed his lips to hers. She felt that tingling sensation again as she closed her eyes and kissed him back.

"Come with me," he whispered as he took her hand and led her up the stairs. He left her standing in the middle of the room while he closed and locked the door. Stepping back over to her, he placed his hands on her waist, grasped the bottom of her sweater and slowly pulled it up and over her head. Then he reached down and began unfastening her jeans. Instinctively, she placed her hands atop his, but looking into his eyes, she could resist no longer. She slid her hands along his arms and, when she reached his shoulders, they kissed again.

Shed of their clothes and snuggled under the same colorful quilt Beth had slept under last November, tender caresses and lingering kisses developed into intimate lovemaking. Exhausted, she lay next to Paul and listened to his breathing. As she shifted slightly, he stirred and spoke to her quietly, making his deep voice even deeper. "I love you, Beth."

So happy she felt as though her heart would burst, she replied, "I love you, too."

CHAPTER 22

Amy Thompson locked the door to her gift shop and headed around the corner toward the bed & breakfast. Usually she stayed open during the whale festival, but this year she and Beth had decided to join the tourists and enjoy the wine and chowder tasting. They had even talked Paul into going with them. Tom, on the other hand, was a lost cause. He loved the wine tasting. Every year he had the same winery set up in his bookstore. That way he got all the free wine he wanted, and it gave him an opportunity to show off his expertise on the subject.

Amy walked into the dining room at the bed & breakfast and noticed that only one table was still occupied. The rest had been cleared, nothing left but the bare wooden tables. In the kitchen, she spotted Beth rinsing dishes and putting them in the dishwasher. Paul was scrubbing a huge cooking pot in the sink, and Clara was putting away the leftover food.

"Aren't you guys ready to go yet?" Amy asked, sitting on the stool by the door.

"Almost," Beth answered. "We just have one last table to clear, and then we'll be done."

For the past two months she'd been spending most of her time building her photography portfolio and helping out at the bed & breakfast. Amy could tell she enjoyed it by the way she bustled about the kitchen, laughing and talking with Paul. Even Clara seemed to like having Beth around, which was amazing. It was a well-known fact that Clara did not tolerate just anyone in her kitchen.

"Pots and pans are all done," Paul said, turning away from the sink. "Just need the last of the dishes and we'll be finished."

"Great, I'll go grab them. Wanna help?" Beth asked Amy.

"Sure, if it'll get us out of here faster."

Grabbing the grey rectangular tubs from under the sink, Beth handed one to Amy. Paul followed them out into the dining room armed with a broom and dustpan. In just a few minutes, the last table was cleared and the floor was swept.

"Now, let's go have some fun," Paul said, taking off his apron and helping Beth out of hers. He hung them on the hooks on the back of the door.

"Are you sure you don't want to come?" Beth asked Clara.

"I'm sure," Clara replied. "Going to my bungalow and put my feet up." Then the short cook disappeared out the back door.

"Where exactly is this chowder tasting?" Beth asked as the trio walked the short distance toward Lansing Street.

"Crown Hall," Paul and Amy answered in unison. "It's actually down by your house," Paul added.

Turning right, they strolled the two blocks to Ukiah, turned left and headed down the hill to the largest meeting hall in Mendocino.

As they walked in the door, the smell of seafood chowder greeted them. "I'm starving," Amy said, looking at the crowd milling around the large room, going from table to table and tasting chowder being ladled from giant pots into the small Styrofoam cups they were holding.

"This is my treat," Paul said pulling out his wallet. "Consider it your wages for the day."

With her own cup and spoon in hand, Amy left Paul and Beth behind and went in search of the perfect chowder. On the third table, she found albacore sandwiches, which she gladly sampled. Wanting to share the delicious fare she had discovered, she scanned the crowd for the other two. She soon spotted them, not far from the front door, feeding bites to each other. Again a pang of jealousy swept over her. "Oh, knock it off," she told herself.

"Excuse me?" inquired a tall man standing next to her. "Did you say something?"

"Uh, no. Sorry." *Oh great!* The familiar heat of embarrassment moved up her neck and into her face. Turning back to the table, she picked up another sandwich and crammed it into her mouth.

"I wouldn't have thought there could be so many different seafood chowders," Beth Braddock admitted after trying only half of what the tasting had to offer.

"Me neither," Paul agreed, "but I still think my favorite is the second one we tried."

"It was really good, wasn't it? How were the mussels?"

"They were okay but not as good as what my mom used to fix. Are you sure you don't want to try some?" he said, offering her one skewered on the end of his fork.

Beth grimaced. "Ugh, positive. After seeing my uncle use them for fish bait, I don't think I could bring myself to eat one. Do you see Amy? I can't find her anywhere."

Paul looked around. "There she is, heading out the

front door. Are you ready to go or do you want to try some more?"

"I've had enough. How about you?"

"I think I'm ready for some wine now. Let's go find Amy and head on over to Tom's."

"I'm right behind you." Beth tossed her cup and spoon into the nearest trashcan. Outside they found Amy sitting on a bench, bent over and holding her stomach with both hands.

"Are you okay?" Beth asked, sitting down next to her.

"Yeah, just had one sandwich too many, I think," Amy said, without looking up.

"Well, come on. I know just the thing for that." Paul held out his hand.

Amy didn't move. "Are you sure you're okay?" Beth asked again. Slowly Amy raised her head. Beth could see tears in her eyes. "What is it?" she asked. "What's wrong?"

Suddenly Amy burst into tears. "I'm sorry," she said when her sobs subsided. "I don't want to spoil our day. Maybe I should just go on home." Amy wiped her eyes with the backs of her hands.

"Don't be silly," Paul said, sitting down on the other side of her. "Now spill it. What's eatin' you?"

"You'll just think I'm being petty."

"No we won't, will we Paul?"

"Absolutely not."

Amy studied the ground. "Lately I've been feeling kind of...well, kind of...I miss having sex!" she blurted.

"Oh geez," Paul whispered, turning away from her and slumping down on the bench.

Beth couldn't believe what she just heard. "Did you say you missed —"

"Yes. I don't mean just the act of sex, but close human contact. Snuggling, holding hands, all that stuff. I never thought about it much before but watching the two of you, I feel like I'm missing out on something that could be really special." Amy sniffed.

"Oh Amy." Beth put an arm around her friend's shoulders. "Have you talked to Tom about this?"

"Yeah, right." She wiped her nose on her sleeve. "Talk to the man who's never getting married. I mean he's great to have dinner with and talk about wine and books, but he's never even touched me, unless you count the time he patted me on the back because I was choking."

Beth leaned forward and looked at Paul. "Would you like Paul to talk to Tom?" she asked. His eyes got big and he shook his head ever so slightly.

"No, this is something I've got to work through for myself," Amy said, taking a deep breath.

Beth frowned at the man as he let out a silent sigh of relief. "Well, come on." She stood, pulling Amy to her feet. "Let's go have some wine. I think you could use some." Arms linked together like the three musketeers, they cut down Woodward Street to Main.

A few minutes later they entered the bookstore and spotted Tom standing in front of the wine table. The wine stewards seemed very amused by the conversation he was having with two guys who were obviously tourists, wearing khaki-colored hiker shorts with multiple pockets, Tommy Hilfiger shirts, floppy hats, and hiking boots with rolled down grey wool socks. One had a camera hanging around his neck and the other had a small pair of binoculars.

After getting their glasses, the trio moved closer to Tom; first to get some wine and second to hear the yarn he was spinning. It was so entertaining that when the tourists stepped away and Tom turned around, they all clapped, including the stewards. Undaunted, Tom took a bow.

"About time you appreciated my vast knowledge of wine," he said, picking up his glass as if to offer a toast. There was laughter and the clinking of glasses. "So how was the chowder tasting?" he asked.

"Delicious," Paul said rubbing his stomach. "And Amy apparently found some yummy sandwiches. Right Amy?" Beth nudged him in the ribs with her elbow.

"Don't remind me," Amy said, glaring at Paul and holding her stomach with her free hand. "I'm hoping this wine will get rid of the bad taste in my mouth."

"Better have some more just to make sure," Tom said, picking up a bottle. Amy held out her glass, and he topped it off.

"Thanks."

"Have you been to any other businesses yet?" Tom asked, refilling his own glass before placing the bottle back on the table.

"Nope, this was our first stop," Beth answered.

"Well, be sure and go by Bessie's candle shop," Tom said. "People have been telling me how good the cabernet is, and I haven't had a chance to get there."

"Well, come with us now," Paul said, throwing his arm around Tom's shoulders. "I'm sure they can get along without you here for a little while."

Tom looked around the bookstore. Both of his temporary clerks were standing behind the counter. There were two people getting wine and a third one was browsing through the books.

"Well, okay," Tom said. He grabbed his wine glass and started out the door with Paul.

Amy slid over to Beth. "Now how did Paul manage that?" she asked. "I've tried for two years to get him out of this store and enjoy some wine with me."

"I guess Paul just has a way with people, convincing

them to do what he wants," Beth replied. *At least he does with me.* Walking alongside Amy, Beth tried to think of a way to help her, but for the moment she had no idea how. Amy was going to have to decide what kind of relationship she wanted and with whom.

When the foursome got to the candle shop, it was packed with people. Tom took the lead and slowly they maneuvered up to the table of wine.

"Well, Tom Miller," the steward said, pouring Tom's glass up to the top. "I was hoping to see you today. How's my favorite customer?"

"Hello, Chris," Tom answered. "I'm just fine. All I've heard today is how good this cabernet is, so I've come to check it out for myself."

"Then my plan worked. You see, I have been telling everyone that if they liked this wine to tell Tom Miller at the bookstore. I knew I wouldn't be able to get away to tell you about it myself, so I let the other folks do it for me."

"Pretty sneaky. So what's so great about this wine?" Tom asked, holding his glass up to the light.

"Have you tasted it?" Chris asked.

"Not yet." Tom took a small sip of the wine. "Man, this is terrific. What's a case of this stuff cost?"

"That's why I wanted to talk to you. They just started bottling this particular batch. It won't be boxed up and ready to sell for a couple of months, but I might be able to pull a few bottles aside until you can come by and pick them up."

"Sounds great. I'll call you when I head your way." Tom finished off his glass, and had Chris fill it up again before leaving the candle shop.

Each place they visited, Tom managed to find someone he knew. Beth was surprised by his vast knowledge of each winery involved in the tasting. After an hour and a half of sampling wine, they made their way back to the bookstore, which was a good thing; she was feeling a little tipsy.

"Well, my lady," Paul began, "shall we away to the inn and make preparations for the evening meal?" Beth wondered if maybe Paul wasn't a lot tipsy.

"My lady?" Amy whispered to Beth. "What's up with that?"

Beth shrugged and moved toward the door. Paul rushed to her side, pulled the door open, and bowed as she walked through. Beth looked back at Amy, watched her roll her eyes, and tried to suppress a giggle. Tom stood near the wine table mid-pour, his eyes wide and his mouth hanging open.

"What was that all about?" Beth asked Paul once they were outside, slipping her arm through his.

He laughed. "Oh nothing. I was just messing with Tom. While we were walking around today, he told me how glad he was that I seemed to be a serious sort of guy that didn't make a fool of himself."

"Well, I think you got a reaction out of him. Did you see the look on his face?"

"Yeah. It was great."

Beth hugged Paul's arm tighter. "You make me laugh, Paul Hayden."

"And you make me happy, Beth Braddock. Happier than I thought possible. I'm so grateful you've come into my life."

CHAPTER 23

Tom Miller laid his garment bag across the bottom of his empty trunk, tossed his toiletry bag in next to it, and slammed the lid. He had his itinerary all set, the usual loop through Sonoma County followed by two or three stops in the Anderson Valley on the way home. The entire trip should take around ten days, and since he was going between the Whale Festival and spring break, business shouldn't be too crazy for his part-time clerk to handle.

He patted his left back pocket and checked his watch. *Time to get on the road.* He debated whether or not to stop by Amy's and say goodbye. Inevitably it would end in a discussion as to why she can't go with him, which he really didn't feel like having. Instead, he decided to drop by Paul's bed & breakfast to grab a latte for the road and whatever pastry Clara may have baked over the weekend.

As he stepped through the front door moments later, the typical din of a meal in progress greeted him. Entering the small dining room, he was surprised to see Amy enjoying a beverage and visiting with Beth as she moved from table to table.

"Hey Tom," Paul called as he turned away from the espresso machine. "Find a spot, and I'll get your usual going."

"You have a 'usual'?" Amy asked, motioning him over to her table.

"Guess so." He pulled out a chair and sat across from her.

"Of course he does," Paul said, placing a huge white mug piled high with foam in front of Tom. "He stops in here at least two or three times a week. Especially around baking days, eh Tom?" Paul clapped him on the back, and Tom offered his sheepish grin.

"Aren't you supposed to be going on your wine run soon?" Amy asked, watching Tom take a sip of his drink.

"Mmphh." He held up his left index finger. "Heading out today," he said as he returned the mug to the table.

Amy frowned and did not reply.

"I just stopped by for a latte and breakfast pastry to eat on the way."

"Clara's made my favorite," Beth said, placing the two coffee decanters she'd been holding back on their warming burners. "Would you like to eat it now or shall I bag it up for you?"

"I was hoping to get an early start..." Tom began. He looked down at his drink and then up at his friends, who were all staring at him. "But I might as well enjoy it now." The others smiled, and Beth hurried through the swinging door into the kitchen. She quickly returned with a muffin bigger than Tom's fist.

"Banana nut," she said, setting the small plate down in front of him. Paul brought over two more lattes, and he and Beth sat in the remaining two chairs at Amy's table.

"Mmm, this is delicious," Tom mumbled around his mouthful of muffin.

"Of course it is," Amy said, "if Clara made it."

"So, going anywhere special this trip?" Paul asked.

"No, just the usual places for my semi-annual restocking. I seemed to have blown through quite a few bottles since my last trip."

"Must have been all our get-togethers," Beth offered.

"That and I gave some as gifts, too."

"Speaking of gifts, I do hope you're picking up some more of that pinot noir I like."

Tom nodded at Paul. "It's at the top of the list. And I contacted Chris. He has a case of that fabulous cabernet set aside."

As Tom finished his breakfast, most of the guests cleared out. The last one left just before Clara pushed through the swinging door, carry two large grey tubs.

"I thought breaktime came after all the dishes were done."

Beth jumped up. "Oh here, let me get those for you, Clara," she said, taking the tubs. As Beth separated them and handed one to Paul, the short chef raised an eyebrow at him before clumping back through the swinging door.

"Time for me to get over to the gift shop before Sandy starts beating the door down," Amy said, standing and pushing her chair up to the table. "Have a good trip," she called over her shoulder as she crossed the dining room. Without another word, she left.

Tom stared after her for several seconds. *That's odd; no fuss, no muss.* Not that he was complaining; it sure beat the heck out of the third degree he usually got. Perhaps the next time...

"Earth to Tom."

"Huh?" Startled, Tom turned around to discover Paul staring at him and Beth nowhere in sight.

"I said looks like you've got good weather for your trip."

"Oh, yeah. The forecast for the next ten days is all sunshine. Should be great." He checked his watch. "Guess I better get on the road." He stood and slid his chair back into place. "See you later."

"Later," Paul replied, getting to his feet and piling dishes into the tub.

Tom strolled down the sidewalk and through the gate, half-expecting to see Amy waiting for him, but she wasn't. He slipped behind the wheel and fired up his Z3. Following Highway 1 south for a few miles, he pulled over at the top of the hill just past Van Damme Beach. Determined to enjoy the sunshine as much as possible, he released the latches that secured the soft top in place and let it drop back into its slot. Then, after making sure the emergency brake was on, he got out and snapped the cover into place. Glancing down onto the small beach, he was surprised to see a section of the guardrail missing, only the short, wooden posts positioned between the roadway and the sheer drop. Shuddering at the thought of a car careening over the edge, he climbed back into his vehicle and continued on his way.

Beth Braddock went through her camera bag. Three rolls of film. She hoped that would be enough. She still had no idea where Paul was taking her. "Pack lots of film and a warm coat," was all he'd told her. But for what? Amy may love this secret stuff, but it made Beth nervous.

She put the bag by the front door and then went into the bedroom. She got a heavy white sweater out of the dresser and pulled it on over her red T-shirt. Then she dug her parka and hiking boots out of the closet and carried them into the living room. She had just finished tying her bootlaces when Paul knocked once on the front door and walked in.

"Good morning. Are you ready to go?" he asked.

"I guess so. Can't you even give me a hint as to where we're going?"

"Nope, you'll figure it out soon enough."

"Let me get Annie chained up and we can go."

"Oh, you can bring her along if you want to. I think she'll like it."

Beth turned to the dog standing in the doorway. "What about it old girl? Do you want to go?" Annie wagged her tail and barked.

"Well, I'll take that as a yes," he said picking up Beth's bag and coat and starting out the door, Beth and Annie close behind him.

Paul put Beth's things into the car. "Come on Annie, let's put you in the back over here." He opened up his door and folded over the seat. It took Annie three tries before she finally managed to get into the back. "Poor old thing. She's getting pretty lame."

"Yeah, I think it's the dampness here. She just isn't as spry as she used to be," Beth said, settling into the passenger seat and buckling up.

Paul started up the Honda Element and pulled away from the curb. In a few minutes they were heading north on Highway 1.

"So where are we going?" Beth asked.

"Uh-huh. Can't tell without spoiling the surprise. Just sit back and relax. We'll be there in about fifteen minutes."

"Fifteen minutes, huh? That puts us in Fort Bragg. Okay, where in Fort Bragg could you be taking me?" Beth sat pondering for a minute. Maybe something was going on at the college. Certain that she wasn't going to get any more information out of Paul, she turned on the radio and began to search for a station she liked.

"Here, try this out," Paul said, sliding a CD into the stereo. Celtic music began to fill the vehicle.

"Where did you get this?" Beth asked.

"The group we listened to the other night was selling them, so I picked up a couple."

Beth sat back and let the music take her, tapping her feet to the sound of the flutes and the rhythm of the drums. "This music makes me want to dance," she said.

"I'll have to keep that in mind." Paul smiled at her.

As he stopped for the traffic light at the junction of Highway 20, the sun began to peek through the clouds. "Looks like it's going to be sunny, at least for a while. I was hoping the visibility would be good today." Before the light changed, he turned east and started up the road that winds its way through the redwoods and towards Willits. "Visibility for what?" Beth asked.

"Not telling," Paul said, turning left onto South Harbor and following it down into the little harbor.

Beth still had no clue why they were there. Not only were all the restaurants closed, they were on the other side of the river. And it was still too early in the morning to watch the fishing boats unload.

Paul pulled into a parking space near the marina. "Now what?" Beth asked.

"Let's grab our stuff and get it aboard Dave's boat."

"Who's Dave?"

"He's an old friend of mine who moved back here last fall. His dad needed help on his fishing boat, and since things weren't working out too good for Dave at the time, he came home to help."

Beth opened her door and stepped out. Paul slid out and freed Annie from the backseat. Glad to be out of the car, she immediately began chasing her nose around the lot.

Beth moved to the rear of the vehicle, threw the strap of her camera bag over her shoulder, and grabbed her coat. Paul, his own duffle bag and jacket in hand, closed up the back of the Element and started toward the docks. Annie fell in at his heels and Beth followed the two of them.

Slowly they weaved their way through the network of docks until Paul stopped in front of a red and white fishing boat. It wasn't the largest one Beth had ever seen, but it was good size. The guy standing on the deck of the boat was the perfect icon of a typical fisherman. He had on a yellow slicker and tall rubber boots. His red curly hair poked out from under the stocking cap he had jammed on his head.

"Morning Dave," Paul called, tossing his duffle and jacket into the boat.

"Hey. Ready to go? Looks like we're going to have great weather."

Paul stepped over to Beth and took her coat and bag. "Looks like. Here, take these would you?" he said, handing them to Dave.

"Sure thing." Dave set her things on the deck, stepped back over to the side and extended his hand. "You must be Beth."

"Good morning, Dave." She took his hand. "Thanks," she said, stepping into the boat. Annie, who had been sitting on the dock, began to whine and paced back and forth. Paul grabbed her collar and led her to the edge of the dock.

"You're next, Annie. Dave, grab her, will you? Not sure she'll be able to make the jump."

"You bet." He wrapped his arms around the dog and placed her in the boat. Then he climbed up the ladder to the bridge. "Go ahead and cast off."

Paul unwound the two huge ropes that were holding the boat in its slip and tossed them on board. Then he jumped down from the dock and, after stowing their stuff in the small cabin, joined Beth and Annie in the bow. The boat glided through the marina and started toward the mouth of the Noyo River. The restaurants that bustled with activity every evening sat dark and silent. As the boat left the harbor, it received a boisterous sendoff from the seals that were stretched out on the rocks.

"Now can you tell me what we're doing?" Beth asked Paul, slipping her arm through his.

"I thought you might like to have some whale photos for your show."

"Whales? You mean we're going out to — what show?" Beth faced Paul.

"Oh, didn't I tell you?" He smiled down at her. "Suzy's looking for someone to display their work for the showing in August. She'd really like to have a photographer."

Beth looked out over the water. "Do you really think my photos are good enough?" she finally asked.

"Beth, how often do you have to put together more photo cards?"

"Well, lots but I just thought it was because I kind of had a corner on the market."

"And because you're a good photographer. I get tons of compliments on the picture of the bed & breakfast."

"I'll think about it, but..."

"Spouts ahead," Dave called from the bridge.

"Better get your camera ready," Paul said. "I'll get it." He disappeared into the cabin and soon returned with Beth's bag. She took it but continued to scan the horizon.

"Oh look, there's a spout," she said, pointing off to the left. "Ooh, there's another one." She dug out her camera and attached the auto wind to the bottom of it. "Don't want to miss anything," she said, grinning at Paul.

Moments later, a huge dark grey back with patches of barnacles on it, emerged from the water right next to the boat. Twin nostrils opened and a double stream of vapor shot up. Beth could feel a light mist covering her face.

"Eww, what are those crawly things?" she asked, pointing at the small crab-like creatures scurrying around the large round barnacles.

"Those are whale lice," Dave called down. "They hang out waiting for flakes of whale skin or other bits of food."

"Gross," Beth said, taking some photos before the whale disappeared below the surface.

"There's a small pod dead ahead." Dave cut the engine. "You might want to come up here for a better view. Looks like there's a baby in the group."

After returning her bag to the small cabin, Beth followed Paul up the narrow, steep ladder to the bridge. "Where are they?" Beth said, trying to steady herself. The small deck pitched back and forth like the Shakin' Shack of a fun house.

"Little more to the right. You can just see their backs coming up out of the water." The boat drifted closer, pushed along by the waves, until Beth could easily see each whale. And there, right in the middle of the group was a baby. It looked like a miniature version of the others and was lying across another whale's back.

Beth took several shots of the whales rolling through the waves with their explosive spouts and their tails lifting high into the air, water streaming off them.

"Each time you see a tail like that," Dave explained, "the whale is diving deeper. And see, each tail has a unique pattern on it." Beth nodded as she continued to snap pictures.

Slowly the pod began to swim away from the boat. "I need to put in another roll of film and this is a good time to do it," Beth said starting for the ladder.

"I'll see if I can find another group that might be a little more active," Dave said, starting the engine again.

The boat lurched forward causing Beth's foot to slip off the top rung. Fortunately she had slung her camera over her shoulder and was able to catch herself before she fell. She made her way down into the little cabin and pulled a new roll of film out of her bag. By the time she got it loaded into the camera, she felt queasy. Stumbling out of the tiny room, she made her way to the bow of the boat. *Just need some fresh air.*

"Beth, come back up here. Dave's found another group," Paul shouted. Beth shook her head and waved him off. She closed her eyes and breathed deeply, hoping the nausea would pass.

"Are you all right?" a deep voice whispered in her ear seconds later, making her jump. She wheeled to find Paul standing right behind her.

"Sorry, didn't mean to startle you," he said.

"Got a little seasick changing the film, but I'll be okay."

"You do look a little green around the gills. Why don't you sit down?" Paul stepped around her and retrieved a small chair from a storage area in the bow. As he turned around, Beth pushed past him.

"Oh my!" She raised the camera and depressed the shutter button. The auto wind hummed and the frames flew through the camera.

"Wow! Did you see that?" Dave shouted from his place at the wheel.

"Sure did. And I got it on film. They should be spectacular shots. Don't you think so, Paul?"

When he didn't answer, Beth turned around and discovered him sprawled on the deck. Annie was standing over him, licking his face.

"All right, all right girl. That's enough," he said, holding his hands up and trying to avoid the dog's slobbery tongue.

"What are you doing down there?" Beth asked him. She could hear Dave laughing above her.

"Apparently I was between a photographer and the perfect shot," Paul said, getting to his feet.

"You mean I..."

Paul nodded.

"Oops, sorry," Beth said. "Are you okay?"

"My face got a good bath," Paul said, looking down at Annie. "Otherwise I'm fine. So, what did I miss?"

"Oh, this whale came straight out of the water and then crashed back down with a gigantic splash!" Beth waved her hands over her head, imitating the spray of water.

"That's called breaching," Dave yelled. "Pretty awesome, huh?"

"I wouldn't know," Paul said brushing himself off.

Beth stepped over to him and gave him a big hug. "I'm really sorry. When I saw that whale coming out of the water, all I could think of was getting a picture."

Paul laughed. "I know. Can't wait to see how they turn out. Are you ready to head back? Clara will be expecting me before too long."

"Sure. I'll get these rolls of film over to Amy's and get them developed." Beth pulled the strap off her neck and stuffed the camera back in the bag. "Then I'll come over and help."

"Sounds like a plan." Paul moved toward the ladder. "Hey Dave, I think we're ready to head in," he said as he got to the top.

"Whatever you say." Dave spun the wheel and the boat began its wide turn. "I didn't see any more pods close by anyhow. It's the tail end of the run, and there are fewer and fewer whales out here. But I'd say it was worth the trip, wouldn't you?" he asked, nodding at Beth, who had just stepped off the ladder and onto the bridge.

"Most definitely. Thanks again for taking us out."

"My pleasure. Besides now Paul owes me a favor, and I know just how he can repay me. It's abalone season, and I need someone to dive with me this weekend. You still have your wetsuit don't you?" he asked Paul.

"Yeah, but it's been a long time since I've done any diving."

"Oh come on, it's like riding a bike. As soon as you get in the water, it'll all come back to you. What do you say?"

"Next weekend, huh?" Paul looked at Beth. "I suppose I can squeeze it into my schedule. When and where?"

"Be at Van Damme State Park around nine o'clock Saturday morning."

"Do I need to bring anything special?"

"Nope, just your wetsuit. I've got an extra pry bar and collection net you can use. This is going to be great." Dave pushed the throttle forward and the boat sped toward shore.

Beth looked toward the approaching land and suddenly shivered.

"Are you cold?" Paul asked, putting his arm around her.

"Not really." She snuggled into his embrace. *Just a bad feeling.*

CHAPTER 24

Beth Braddock began to feel uneasy again as Paul swung into Van Damme Beach and pulled into a parking space that faced the ocean. The early morning fog had burned off, and the sun shone down on the dozen other vehicles already parked there. The beach was dotted with abalone fishermen getting ready to dive for the prized shellfish.

"Doesn't look like he's here yet," Paul said. He turned off the engine and climbed out. As he reached the back of the Honda, his friend pulled in next to him.

"Looks like a great day to go diving," Dave said, dropping the tailgate of his old Ford pickup. Dents and patches of rust covered its light blue body.

"Good morning Dave," Beth called as she got out of the small SUV.

"Hey, Beth. Come to check out the action."

"Wouldn't miss it." She joined Paul at the back of the vehicle, who was balanced on one leg, pulling on his wetsuit.

"I'll go set up base camp and come right back." She reached into the back of the Honda and pulled out her bag, an old quilt, and the picnic basket Clara had packed for them. Picking out a spot halfway to the water, she spread the quilt on the sand, placed the rest of the things on it, and walked back to the car.

Still trying to get into his wetsuit, Paul had only gotten it pulled up as far as his hips. His face was covered with perspiration, and his brow was furrowed with concentration. Dave, already dressed in his own wetsuit, was leaning against his pickup, obviously trying not to laugh.

"Having some trouble?" Beth asked. Paul flashed his green eyes at her. Having seen that look before, she moved over by Dave.

"Tell me again how this works," she said as she continued to watch Paul struggle.

"We free dive to where the abalone are, pry them off with a pry bar, and put them into a net," Dave explained.

"Sounds easy enough. How long will you be out there?"

"Oh, probably about thirty to forty minutes. That should be enough time to get our limits. Much longer than that and a diver could get hypothermia. The water is pretty cold." Beth shuddered as a shiver ran down her spine.

Paul, finally zipped into his wetsuit and with his flippers and mask in hand, stepped over to Dave's truck.

Too bad he's going underwater; he looks good in that thing.

"Okay, I'm ready," he said. "Where's my pry bar and net?"

Dave reached into the back of his truck and pulled out matching pry bars. "I've got this marked so you can use it to measure the abalone," he said, handing one of them to Paul. "And here's a net." Then he grabbed his own mask and flippers, and the two of them started toward the water.

Beth walked along with them as far as the quilt, where she sat down and watched them continue across the beach. When they reached the water's edge, they put on their flippers and masks, hooked the nets to their diving belts, and waded into the surf until they disappeared from sight.

Beth checked her watch; it was just after nine thirty. *Might as well get comfortable; it'll be awhile.* She lay back and let the sun's warmth embrace her.

Waking from a light sleep, Beth opened her eyes and slowly became aware of her surroundings. Looking at her watch, she realized forty-five minutes had gone by. She sat up and looked toward the parking area. Seeing no one she knew, she got up and walked toward the ocean.

Abalone fishermen were materializing out of the surf and making their way to a temporary weigh-in station set up in the far corner of the parking lot. Most of them had something in their nets. Further on down the beach, she spotted Dave. He had just taken off his flippers and was making his way up the shore. Beth hurried toward him.

"Where's Paul?" she asked when she got close enough.

"He's not here?" Dave frowned at her. "We got separated and I just assumed he'd already come in."

"I haven't spotted him if he did." She felt certain he was not on shore.

"Let's get these guys checked in," Dave said, holding up his net, "and have a look around." He started toward his truck. Beth took one last look at the Pacific, half-expecting Paul to walk out of the water, and then started after Dave. She tripped twice, looking at the faces in the growing crowd instead of where she was going. Checking her watch again, she began to worry. Paul had been gone for over an hour.

While Dave dealt with the guy from the Department of Fish and Game, Beth shifted from one foot to the other, her eyes constantly searching the shoreline. Finally, in the distance, she saw someone that looked vaguely familiar walking out of the waves.

She took off running, hoping it was Paul and not some stranger. She was amazed at how quickly she moved. As she got closer, Beth knew it was Paul but something was wrong. He had his arms wrapped around his midsection like he was protecting himself. She could see part of his chest through a large gaping hole in his wetsuit. When she reached him, she threw her arms around him. "What happened to you? I've been so worried about you." Beth stepped to his side and put her arm around his waist. "When Dave came in alone, I was afraid something had happened to you."

"I have quite a story to tell you, but first I need to get this damn wetsuit off. I'm freezing."

Beth could feel his whole body trembling. "Come on. I've got just the thing," she said, leading him to the spot where the quilt lay on the ground. She suspected Paul was suffering from hypothermia. She'd had it before herself as a young girl after swimming in a cold mountain lake. What he needed was warmth, and quick. "Here, turn around and let's get you out of this thing." Beth tugged on the cord attached to the zipper and yanked the wetsuit off his shoulders and down around his knees, leaving Paul standing there in his red Speedo. Then she snatched up the quilt and wrapped it around him, making sure the side that had been warmed by the sun was against him.

"Oh man, that feels so good," he said through chattering teeth.

"Good. Get out of this thing." She stepped on his wetsuit so he could pull his legs free. "And let's get you back to the car. There's coffee in this thing," she said picking up the picnic basket. "That'll help warm you up on the inside." She grabbed her bag and reached for the discarded wetsuit.

"Leave it. We'll come back for it," Paul said, starting

for the parking lot. Beth ran to the car, opened the passenger side door of the Honda Element and had Paul sit down. Then she poured him a cup of hot coffee out of the thermos.

"Well, look what the tide washed in," Dave said, walking up. He dropped his abalone into an ice chest in the back of his truck. "Where the hell did you go?"

Paul shook his head. "You're not going to believe what happened out there. I was hassled by a sea lion."

Dave started to laugh. "You were what?"

"I'm not kidding. I was hassled by a goddam sea lion." Paul took another sip of coffee. "I was having a hard time finding abalone that were big enough, so I kept moving down the shoreline. Pretty soon I noticed there was this sea lion following me. I didn't think anything about it until it grabbed my flipper."

"Your flipper? You mean it tried to bite you?" Dave asked. He leaned against his pickup and folded his arms across his chest.

"Yup. Tore that thing right off my foot. So there I was, only one flipper trying to get back to the beach, but before I got very far that damn sea lion swam right in front of me. No matter which way I turned, it stayed in front of me like it was trying to herd me." Paul took another sip of coffee. "Then it started charging at me. I kept swinging at it with the pry bar but could never hit it. Next thing I know it's grabbed hold of the net and is pulling me away from the beach into deeper water. At one point it dragged me over an outcropping where something caught my wetsuit and tore it open. When that cold water hit my chest, it was all I could do to keep from gasping and filling my lungs with water. Finally, I managed to reach down and undo my diving belt. The sea lion kept going and I exploded onto the surface. Then I swam as fast as I could and didn't look back."

Dave shook his head. "You know, I've heard stories about rogue sea lions attacking divers like that but I always thought it was a bunch of bullshit. Leave it to you, Paul." He chuckled. "Well, I'm glad you got away, but I suppose you lost my pry bar."

"Glad to know you're so concerned about me," Paul said. "Your pry bar's not lost; it's just submerged somewhere out there," he said, pointing toward the ocean with his thumb. "And I'm sure that sea lion would be happy to show you where it is."

"Well, I'm relieved you're safe," Beth said, tousling his hair with her hand. She bent down and gave him a long, deep kiss. "No more diving for you. I can't stand the stress. Now, what do you say we head home?"

"Sounds good to me. You drive." Paul swung his legs inside and pulled the door shut.

Beth walked around the car to the driver's side. "Dave, would you mind getting Paul's wetsuit? I want to get him into a hot shower." Dave's right eyebrow arched. "I mean I want to heat him up." Both of Dave's eyebrows went up, and Beth blushed.

Dave laughed. "Yeah, I'll get it. See you later."

Beth got in and started the engine. Watching Dave stroll out onto the beach, she realized she was about to do something she hadn't done for a long time. Slowly she reached out her hand and placed it on the gearshift. As if reading her mind, Paul placed his hand on hers.

"You'll do just fine," he said smiling at her.

Giving him a faint smile in return, Beth put the car in reverse and slowly backed out of the space. Then she slipped it into first gear, let out a slow breath, and inched toward Highway 1. It wasn't until they crossed the Big River Bridge that she began to relax.

"Grab my pants and shirt out of the back would you?"

Paul said when they got back to the bed & breakfast. Beth didn't answer but sat looking straight ahead. "Beth, did you hear me?"

"Uh-huh. I was just imagining you going in like you are. Without the quilt of course."

"Very funny. Now get my clothes."

"What a party pooper," Beth said, getting out of the car.

"Come on in, and we'll have our picnic after I get cleaned up."

While Paul showered, Beth set out the food on the small table in the patio. It wasn't long until he joined her, dressed in faded jeans and a tight-fitting black pullover, which he wore with the sleeves pushed up.

"Feeling better?" she asked.

"Much. I've never been so cold in my life. I'm just glad that stupid animal wasn't more aggressive." Paul shuddered.

"You ought to write about what happened and send it off to some adventure magazine. I bet one of them would buy it."

"Oh, I don't know if anybody..." Paul stopped and looked her in the eye. "Tell you what. I'll write the story and send it off, if you'll put together a showing of your photographs."

Beth opened her mouth and then shut it again. *Why not. It might actually be fun.* "Okay," she said, holding out her hand. "It's a deal."

"Terrific," he said as they sealed the deal with a handshake. "I'll help anyway I can, and I know Amy will too." Paul took a huge bite of his sandwich. "Are you ready for tonight?" he asked around the mouthful of food.

"I have to stop by the store on the way home and pick

up some faster film. There won't be much light from the full moon."

"Are Amy and Sandy coming with us?"

Beth laughed. "Amy's in but not Sandy. Apparently she has a thing about cemeteries.

"Too bad." He took another bite. "I think it's going to be quite an adventure. Should I pick you up?"

"Sure. It might be a little unsettling trying to walk home in the dark afterwards."

"You could always spend the night here." Paul winked at Beth over his mug of coffee.

"Oh yeah, like that would be safe."

CHAPTER 25

The moon bathed the cemetery in a silvery light, making the ancient headstones and marble figures glow. Beth Braddock wrapped her jacket more tightly around her before reaching over and taking hold of Paul's hand. "This is kind of scary isn't it?" she whispered.

"Yeah, isn't it cool?"

"No," Amy replied as she pulled the hood of her sweatshirt further over her head. "The hair on the back of my neck has been standing up on end since we got here."

Beth laughed as she released Paul's hand and continued down the row of gravesites, taking pictures of the more unusual markers. She already had some great photographs; one headstone even had a gargoyle perched on top of it.

Just ahead, the rest of the group was absorbed in the historical information the guide was sharing about the current residents of the graveyard. The tour was part of the Mendocino Heritage Days celebration and, over the last few days, Beth had learned a lot about the area. But she'd never imagined herself walking around in a cemetery — at night — by the light of a full moon. *Good thing I don't believe in werewolves.*

"Come with me," Paul said, "if you want to see something interesting."

"What is it?" Beth asked, following him.

"I'll show you. It's just over here."

"But what about the rest of the tour?" Amy pointed at the others in the group as they moved to the next row.

"It'll just take a few minutes and then we'll rejoin them." Paul led the way toward a redwood tree. Under its immense canopy was a smaller holly tree, just like the one in front of the bed & breakfast. A circular rod-iron fence enclosed the burial site, and inside, next to the tree, a large stone cross bore the name "Lucile Hayden."

"Who's this?" Amy asked, walking around the gravesite.

"Have I ever told you about my crazy great-aunt?"

"No."

"Well, she's the one that bought the bed & breakfast, and this is where she is buried."

"And I suppose there's some significance to each of the things here," Beth said, raising her camera and snapping a few shots.

"Of course." Paul stepped over to the fence and placed his hand on one of the spear-like pickets. "This fence was placed in a circle to protect her from the undead."

"Sounds logical in a cemetery," Beth said, stepping back and taking one more picture of the grave.

"The holly tree is to ward off evil spirits."

"Evil spirits, huh?" Amy muttered, glancing over one shoulder and then the other.

Beth giggled. "Not to be confused with the undead?"

Paul chuckled. "Exactly! And the cross is to protect her from vampires."

"Vampires?" Amy whispered as she pressed her hands to her throat.

"I can't believe your family actually went to all this trouble," Beth said.

"Oh, they didn't. She had all this stuff done when she

first moved here. She didn't want to have to trust anyone else to do it for her."

"I'd be willing to bet that if she were alive today, she'd have everything wrapped in aluminum foil." Amy suggested.

"Aluminum foil?" Beth frowned at her.

"Yeah. Haven't you ever met one of the crazy old ladies that wraps everything in foil? You know, to keep out the gamma rays or something like that? I'd even be willing to bet Sandy has things wrapped in foil."

Beth thought about the strange old woman who lived in the tiny house down the street from her childhood home. She had always wondered why there was foil on all the windows. *Too bizarre for me.*

"Are your parents here, too?" Amy asked, looking around.

"No, this cemetery has been full for a long time. My folks are buried in the one down by Little River. Come on, let's go see what the group's up to."

"Uh actually, I think I'm going to take off," Amy said, pointing back the way they had come. "This has been fun, but..." She looked around again. "I had a busy day, and I'm sure tomorrow will be just as busy." She took a couple of steps, stopped and turned around. "Besides, I'd rather quit now before I really get the bejabers scared out of me." She started off again in the direction of her parked car. "Night," she called over her shoulder.

"Night," Beth and Paul replied in unison.

Then he put his arm around Beth's waist and pulled her in close. "When we're through here," he began, "let's head back to my place for some wine and a small cozy fire. In fact, you should just stay the night."

"My, you are persistent, and it sounds tempting, but

I don't want to leave Annie out all night. Her old bones couldn't take it."

"Then we'll go get her and bring her along. She's always welcome to spend the night, just like her master."

"You're quite the silver-tongued devil, aren't you?" Beth said, tilting her face up to look at him.

Paul tightened his embrace and, placing one hand on the back of her head, gave her a long sensuous kiss, his tongue exploring her mouth. Beth felt her body go limp, held up only by Paul's strong arms. "Only around you," he said when they parted.

*　　*　　*

As light began to creep into the room, Beth lay in the brass bed and listened to Paul's slow, regular breaths. She turned her head and watched as he slept, one arm resting on the pillow over his head and the other across his waist.

Without making a sound, she stole out of bed and tiptoed across the floor to the window. Wisps of fog were swirling around the house. *This is perfect.* She quickly slipped into her jeans, the cold material making her shiver. Annie raised her head and whimpered. "Not this time Girl," Beth whispered to her. "You stay here with Paul." The old dog thumped her tail a couple of times, put her head back down on her paws, and closed her eyes. Beth pulled her shirt on and ran her fingers through her hair. Grabbing her jacket and shoes, she stepped out into the hallway and quietly pulled the door closed behind her. She finished dressing on the way down the stairs, grabbed her camera out of its bag under the counter, and went out the front door.

The fog had settled in, giving everything a ghostly appearance. Beth hurried along the four blocks back to the cemetery, anxious to take all the pictures she wanted before the fog burned off. With any luck she would finish and be back to the bed & breakfast before Paul woke up.

Amy Thompson looked at the crowd of people milling around the gift shop. Busy mornings like these made her smile all the way to the bank. Sandy was processing one batch of photos after another in the developing machine, which left Amy to handle the customers alone. *Wish she'd hurry up; I'm dying to see the pictures.* Beth was so excited to share her news when she dropped the film off this morning; she had finally agreed to have a showing of her photographs!

A blood-curdling scream vibrating through the store jolted Amy from her thoughts. She looked up half-expecting to see a hooded gunman or a large poisonous snake slithering through the store. What she did see was a store full of startled customers staring at Sandy, who stood absolutely still with her hands clamped over her mouth and the color drained from her face.

Amy moved down the counter toward her, noticing out of the corner of her eye that most of the customers were heading in the opposite direction toward the front door. Before Amy could reach her, Sandy began backing away from the photo machine, her breathing rapid and shallow.

"Sandy, are you all right?" she asked when she was close enough.

"There's something — someone — something wrong. An unhappy soul!" Sandy pointed at the pictures scattered on the floor. "I have to go. I can't stay here. I need an herbal tea, right away." Hurrying into the backroom, she grabbed her things, and then ran the full length of the store and out the door. The few customers that had stayed after the initial outburst were close behind her.

All alone in the store, Amy reached down and picked up the photos. Slowly she thumbed through the stack. The pictures were quite clear, even in the reduced light, and they had a certain eeriness to them. Finally she came to one that must have unnerved Sandy. It was a shot of a circular fence enclosing a tree and large cross. But something else was there, between the tree and cross. A hazy white figure seemed to be floating above the ground. Amy thumbed through the rest of the pictures, watching for that same smudge or blemish but found nothing. *Wait until Beth sees this.* She slid the pictures into an envelope, stepped to the phone, and dialed her number.

Tom Miller laid his garment bag across the two shipping containers with Styrofoam inserts he'd scored on his third stop between Calistoga and St. Helena. One was completely full and the other still had a least half of its slots available. He'd spent the last six days weaving his way south between Highway 128 and the Silverado Trail, visiting his favorite wineries and selecting their choice wines.

As he slammed the trunk lid into place, he noticed an older model, white Taurus parked across the street from the motel where he was staying. Ordinarily, he didn't pay attention to vehicles around him, but he was certain he'd seen this one numerous times on his trip.

The crack in the windshield combined with the missing hubcap was conspicuous enough, but the effigy decorated with baby yellow carnations dangling from the rearview mirror was unmistakable. And although he'd never seen anyone driving it, the car always seemed to be parked nearby. *As if the car itself is stalking me!* Chiding himself for being foolish, he slid in behind the wheel and pulled onto Highway 12, headed for Santa Rosa.

CHAPTER 26

A my Thompson scanned the horizon as the sun inched its way toward the Pacific. The breeze that had ruffled the headland grass earlier had grown into a blustery wind, making her appreciate the heavier jacket she'd slipped on before leaving her house.

"Has Sandy recovered yet?" Beth asked as they continued along the trail.

"I think so, but she wouldn't even come back to the shop until you picked up the pictures. They totally freaked her out." Amy hesitated. "Do you think that might have been the ghost of Paul's great-aunt?" She didn't actually believe in ghosts, but what other explanation could there be?

"I don't know. I guess it could be possible, but it will definitely be a conversational piece at the showing." Beth sat down on one of the benches strategically placed along the trail.

"No kidding," Amy said, sitting down next to her. "I want you to know that I'm so excited about your show. What changed your mind?"

Beth smiled. "Paul and I have an agreement. I'm showing my photographs, and he has to write about his mishap with the sea lion and see if some magazine will publish it."

"That certainly was weird, wasn't it? If he hadn't managed to get away..."

"Stop!" Beth said. "I don't even want to think about what might've happened. I'm just thankful he got away."

"Me too." They sat watching the waves break and roll toward shore.

"So are you — have you..." Beth began, ending the silence that had settled over them.

Amy turned toward her and frowned. "Have I what?"

"Well, the other day you said you were..." Beth hesitated. "That is to say, you said you missed —"

"Oh that." Amy grimaced. "Yeah, I was pretty pathetic that day wasn't I. I hope I didn't embarrass Paul too much, blurting out my feelings like that."

"Oh no," Beth said, shaking her head. "I'm sure he's forgotten all about it." She waited a few seconds before continuing. "I was just wondering — have you decided what kind of relationship you want with Tom?"

Amy contemplated Beth's question. *What do I want?* Frustrating as he could be at times, she considered Tom a friend and would continue to do so, but as far as an intimate relationship, she was fairly certain she would have to look elsewhere. As she opened her mouth to answer, a siren blared. She looked back toward the fire hall and watched the massive red fire truck, with its wailing siren and flashing lights, pull through the gigantic door and turn toward Main Street. "I don't see smoke anywhere. Do you?"

Beth shook her head. "Maybe it's going to help with a fire somewhere else," she offered. "When did you say Tom was coming home?"

Amy checked her watch. "He thought he'd be back by five."

"That was half an hour ago."

"He probably got so involved in a discussion about wine, he lost track of the time."

"Has he texted you?"

"Don't know. I left my phone on its charger."

"Let's walk over to your place and check it, if you want. Or you could call him and see where he is."

"Good idea. I'll make us some tea to have on the porch."

The two of them left the vantage point and strolled back along the trail. They didn't get very far before another siren could be heard in the distance. As the sound drew closer, Amy got a strange feeling in the pit of her stomach. She turned toward Mendocino, straining to see what rescue vehicle was coming down the highway. Finally, on the other side of the tiny bay, she caught a glimpse of an ambulance speeding south on Highway 1.

"Beth, I have a bad feeling about this, but I'm not sure why. Tom's such a good driver but..." Amy's stomach felt like it had lead in it. "Want to go for a ride?" she asked.

"A ride?"

"Just down the highway. If there's nothing by the time we get to Albion, we'll turn around and come back." Beth hesitated and looked toward her house. Amy followed her gaze. "Please, Beth. I'm sure Annie's asleep on the porch, and we'll be back before she misses us."

"Okay," Beth said. "Let's go."

They sprinted toward Amy's house and her yellow VW Bug, which she had started and in reverse before Beth could close her door. She backed out of the driveway, slammed the car into first gear, and took off down the road. She rounded the corner by Beth's house and sped toward Highway 1.

The faster the car went the faster her heart beat. She couldn't shake the bad feeling she had. As the VW maneuvered around the sharp turn that drops down toward Van Damme Beach, Amy could see the flashing lights of the emergency vehicles along the edge of the cliff on the other side. Trying to find a place to pull over, she caught only glimpses of what was going on.

"Oh Amy, look," Beth exclaimed, pointing to the base of the cliff that dropped down onto the beach. "Isn't that Tom's car?"

Amy slammed on the brakes and swerved toward the side of the road. There, resting on its roof with its wheels in the air, was a metallic blue car — just like Tom's.

Amy felt the air rush out of her lungs. Unable to drive around the jumble of cars ahead of them, she jumped out of the small yellow car and started running. By the time she reached the top of the hill, her lungs were burning and her legs were shaking. *This has got to be a bad dream.*

She stumbled toward where the car had obviously left the road, become airborne and plunged over the side. Just as she was about the reach the edge, someone grabbed her arm.

"Ma'am, you'll have to stay back. It's not safe. The car has loosened the ground and it's unstable."

Amy turned around to find a young highway patrol-man holding onto her, and she could see herself in the dark lenses of his aviators.

"I need to know where the driver of that car is," Amy demanded, pointing over the side.

"If you'll just calm down and step over here with me..." he began.

"No, you don't understand." She pulled her arm free from his grasp. "Where's the driver? Where's Tom?" Amy shouted, her voice growing higher and louder. "Tom!" she screamed.

"Amy?"

She spun around but couldn't tell who had called her name.

"Over here. I'm over here."

Finally, she spotted a man moving away from the back of the ambulance. He had a large white bandage wound around his head and his tattered shirt was covered with dirt and blood. He stepped toward her with his arms extended. "Omigod, Amy. Am I glad to see you!"

Amy let out a little shriek as she ran to meet him. "Oh, Tom," she said as they embraced each other. "I got this weird feeling that something was wrong, and when I saw the car I knew I had lost..." Amy began crying hysterically and Tom tightened his arms around her.

"Shhh. Don't cry. I'm here and I'm all right. Just some cuts and bruises." Tom continued to hold Amy tightly and gently rocked her back and forth. "When I got up off the ground and saw where the car had gone, I realized how lucky I was — I am. Amy," he said pulling back, gently holding her head in his hands, and peering into her eyes, "now I realize how important you are to me. How much I need you, want to be with you. Amy, I love you and want to marry you."

"Oh, Tom. I love you too."

He pulled her in close again, and when Amy felt his mouth on hers, she was aware of a pulling sensation deep in her belly; a feeling she had not experienced for much too long.

The moment Amy had leapt from the vehicle, Beth Braddock yanked on the emergency brake. Then she reached over, turned off the engine, and pulled the key out of the ignition. By the time she had locked the car and started down the hill, Amy was practically at the top on the other side. *Please God, let Tom be okay.*

When Beth finally made her way to the scene of the

accident, she couldn't find Amy anywhere. She moved further out on the point, avoiding the place where the car actually went over, until she could get close enough to the edge to look down at the water and see the car.

Visions from another time of another car, almost completely submerged, flashed in her mind. Suddenly Beth's ears began to buzz and her vision started to dim. She managed to take a step backward before feeling her knees buckle. But instead of hitting the ground, an arm encircled her waist and steadied her on her feet.

As her head cleared, she turned expecting to see a fireman. Instead she found herself looking into a pair of green eyes that had become so familiar.

"Oh Paul," she said, throwing her arms around his neck. "We think that's Tom's car, but I've lost Amy."

"She's with him over there." He pointed toward the myriad of flashing lights.

"Is he all right?"

"Yeah. Looks like he's kind of banged up, but he's on his feet."

"Thank God," Beth scanned the crowd and spotted Tom and Amy at the back of a blue and white ambulance. She released Paul and stepped back. "How did you know where I was?"

"After the first siren, Clara switched on her scanner. When they gave the location of the accident, I stepped out on the porch and saw the two of you fly by, so I hopped in the Honda and followed you."

"You always seem to be coming to my rescue."

"Just doing my knightly duty, my lady," he said, sweeping his hands out from his sides and bowing. "Now, shall we wander over and find out just what happened to old Tom?"

Hand in hand, they started toward the ambulance.

"Looks like he's having a disagreement with one of the paramedics," Paul said as they got closer.

Beth had to agree. Tom had his arms crossed in front of his chest and was shaking his head while one of the paramedics gestured toward the open doors of the ambulance.

"I told you I don't need to go with you," he was saying as they walked up. "You bandaged my head. I'll be fine."

"But sir," the first paramedic began, "you really should let a doctor check you out. You could have a fracture or internal bleeding."

"Oh, please. I took a roll in the dirt and cut my head. I'm fine."

"Bill," the second paramedic said. "If the guy doesn't want to go, we can't force him. Just have him sign the form that says he refused treatment and let's get out of here. I'm starving."

"Fine." Bill pulled a clipboard out of the back of the ambulance and held it out to Tom. "But I think you're making a big mistake."

"Duly noted," Tom said, signing his name on the form and handing the clipboard back.

The paramedic shook his head, tore off Tom's copy and handed it to him. After tossing the clipboard back into the ambulance and slamming the doors, he moved to the front of the vehicle and climbed in on the passenger side. As soon as he was settled, the ambulance swung around and headed back the way it had come.

CHAPTER 27

Tom Miller crumpled up the piece of pale yellow paper the paramedic had given him and shoved it into his pocket.

"So what the hell happened, Tom?" Paul asked.

"I was wondering that myself." A young highway patrolman approached the group. Tom recognized him as the one who had helped him before the ambulance arrived. He removed his sunglasses and slid them into the pocket of his uniform. His gold name tag pinned to the outside of it identified him as Officer Crawford. "Now that you're all patched up, I was hoping you could tell me what happened."

Tom shrugged as he shook his head. "I'm not really sure. I'd just reached Highway 1 and headed north when I noticed there was a white car following me. At first I didn't think anything of it until I realized it was the same Ford Taurus I'd seen on my trip."

"Are you sure it was the same vehicle?"

"Well, I'm not positive, but it looked like it had the same crack in the windshield. I couldn't tell if the one following me was missing a hubcap but..."

"On the front driver's side?" Paul asked.

Tom frowned as he glanced sideways at his friend. "Yeah. How do you know that?"

"Because I passed a car matching that description at

the top of the hill over there," he said, pointing across Van Damme Beach. "It was parked on the side of the road, but no one was in it."

"Okay, so this vehicle was following you," Officer Crawford said, writing in the small notebook he'd pulled from his hip pocket, "but how did your car end up going over the edge?"

"That's where I'm a little fuzzy. I remember braking to negotiate the turn and then, bam! Next thing I know, my car is sliding sideways toward the open spot in the guardrail. All I could think of was to get out, so I undid my belt as I opened the door and jumped."

"So then the other vehicle ran into you?" The officer pointed his pen at Paul. "And you think you saw that same car parked on the side of the road just north of here. Did you happen to notice the license plate?"

"No, but I'm pretty sure there was damage to the front end, now that I think about it," Paul said.

"Okay, got it. I'll check and see if it's still there. Otherwise, I'll radio in an APB and see if it turns up somewhere." He finished scribbling something into his notebook before shoving it back into his hip pocket. "I've got your contact information, and I'll let you know if anything turns up." He dug a small card out of his front shirt pocket and handed it to Tom. "In the meantime, call me if you think of anything else." Then he turned on his heel and strode toward his cruiser, which he'd parked diagonally across the scenic highway, using it as a roadblock.

As the remaining emergency vehicles turned off their flashing lights and headed back to their respective quarters, the four friends maneuvered closer to the edge and peered down at the two men from a towing business in Fort Bragg who were trying to right Tom's car and get it off the section of beach that had been exposed during low tide.

"If they don't work a little faster," Paul said, "they're gonna have to contend with the rising surf."

"You know," Tom said, rubbing his left shoulder. "I could care less about the car. I've got excellent insurance. But the wine..."

"Wine?" Paul asked.

"I had three cases of wine in my trunk. And now it's gone!" His voice caught a little.

Paul stood silently for a few seconds. "Are you sure you lost all of it? Isn't it possible a bottle or two might've survived?"

Tom shook his head. "I don't see how. I mean, nearly all of them were packed in shipping cases but..." He looked down at the beach again. "My car's upside down!" The other three looked down at the wreckage.

"Yeah," Paul sighed. "I suppose you're right."

They continued watching as the cable that had been attached to the undercarriage of Tom's car became taut and slowly pulled it to its upright position. The windshield was completely flattened over the seats, and the hood and front fenders were a crumpled mess.

"Well, anybody want to give me a ride?" Tom asked, turning away from the recovery going on below him. "I seem to be without a means of transportation."

"Come on," Amy said. "Let's get you home and out of those clothes." She took hold of Tom's arm, and holding it tightly, started down the hill.

Tom glanced at Paul, who raised both eyebrows for just a second and grinned.

"Amy," Beth called, "you might need these." She pulled the VW's keys out of her pocket and held them up.

"Oh, Beth." Amy's eyes widened. "I forgot we came together." For a moment she looked distressed.

"Don't worry," Paul said, taking the keys from Beth and walking them over to her. "I'll make sure she gets home."

Amy relaxed and beamed at him. "Thanks. You're a dear." She latched onto Tom's arm again, and they continued down the hill. When they reached the entrance to the state beach, Tom stopped and watched as his car was pulled across the rocks and sand toward the waiting tow truck.

"Maybe you shouldn't watch," Amy suggested, tugging on his arm.

"Yeah, maybe you're right." But he didn't move — couldn't move. He felt compelled to witness the drama as it unfolded, like a book by a favorite author that he couldn't put down.

"Hold up a second," one of the men called to the other as he followed along behind the wounded car, balancing the armload of debris that had been left behind. "I've gotta put this junk somewhere."

The man operating the winch shut it down and strolled over to the wreck. "Well, there's no way to slide it in under that crushed windshield. Did you try the doors?"

"Won't open."

"How about the trunk?" He stepped to the back of the car and pushed the trunk release button. "Hells bells, there's no room in here for another thing. Best just dump that stuff on top of the windshield for now."

Tom craned his neck, hoping to catch a glimpse of his payload, but the angle was wrong and he couldn't make out the extent of the damage to the boxes. "Be right back," he said, slipping his arm from Amy's grasp.

"Tom! What are you doing?" she demanded as she hurried after him.

"I just want to see if anything survived." He'd almost reached the car when the man who had been carrying the armload of junk placed both hands on the trunk and was about to slam it shut. "Hold up there a second," Tom called. "Just want to take a look at those boxes."

"No can do," the man said. "This here's private property and — hey aren't you the guy that crashed this ride?" He gestured toward Tom's head with his chin.

"Uh, yeah." Tom reached up and rubbed the large white bandage that was wrapped around his head.

"You were mighty lucky to walk away with just a bump on the head, mister."

"Yeah lucky," Tom mumbled. He was still trying to see if any of the cases of wine he'd so carefully packed in the trunk were still intact, but his garment bag completely hid them from view. "Here, take this." He wriggled it free and thrust it at Amy. Then, he opened the flaps of the center cardboard box and pulled off the top half of the Styrofoam insert, revealing the butt ends of twelve wine bottles. "And this," he said, shaking it at her. With trembling hands, he slowly pulled one out of its sleeve. "It's not broken!" he exclaimed. "Look Amy, it's not broken." He held it out for her to inspect. "Run get your car, so we can get these boxes home and check out the rest of them." He replaced the bottle of wine, took the insert from her and slipped back into place. "Wouldn't it be wonderful if none of them were broken?"

"Yeah — just wonderful," she murmured.

Amy Thompson swung the garment bag over her shoulder like an enormous serape and trudged toward the entrance. "I can't believe he's so worried about that damn wine," she mumbled to herself. "Who am I kidding? He'll never change."

"Amy?" It was Beth. She and Paul had just reached the

Van Damme Beach on the way back to his car. "What on earth are you doing? And where's Tom?"

Amy motioned over her shoulder with her thumb. "Rescuing his precious wine. He sent me to fetch my car, so we can haul it home and see how many bottles managed to survive the crash."

Paul looked toward the wrecked car. "You mean they all didn't get broken?"

"Well at least one was okay when he looked inside one of the boxes," she said, continuing on her way to the VW Bug she'd hurriedly pulled to the side of the road and was now the only vehicle left and slightly blocking part of Highway 1.

"That's amazing," he said as he and Beth fell into step with Amy. "I'd like to know how that happened myself."

Amy glared at him. "Oh, I'm sure it will be the topic of conversation for weeks to come." Having reached her vehicle, she unlocked the door, slid in behind the wheel, and slammed the door. Then she started the engine and sat with it idling for almost a minute, toying with the idea of just going home, before throwing it into first gear and driving down the hill to the entrance of Van Damme Beach.

Paul stands on the sidewalk in front of the gallery, watching for Beth to come up the hill. Suddenly, the screeching of tires makes a horrible sound, and a couple walking by turns around and looks back down the hill they have just climbed. Their exclamations of "Oh my God," come up the hill toward the gallery. The man shouts at Paul. "Call an ambulance. Someone has just been hit."

Paul starts toward the hill at a dead run. As he reaches the top, he looks down the road and sees the crumpled heap of the person who has been mowed down by a car. A few more steps closer, he recognizes the victim and tries to run faster, but his legs are heavy and hard to move. Finally, he reaches the place where Beth is lying in the middle of the road.

He kneels down next to her, checking for breathing and a pulse. A few minutes pass, and the siren of an approaching ambulance can be heard. It barrels down the road and comes to an abrupt halt next to them. Paul moves to Beth's head as the paramedics begin their assessment of her damaged body. After placing the neck brace on her, they lay her onto a gurney and load her into the ambulance. He tries to climb in, but is not allowed to go. Watching the ambulance turn left at the next corner and begin its journey to Mendocino Coast District Hospital, he yells, "No!"

Startled awake by his own voice, Paul was relieved to discover it was only a dream, albeit a very bad dream. He turned on his side and studied the sleeping woman next to him. Smiling, he reached out and stroked her highlighted hair before falling back to sleep.

CHAPTER 28

Tom Miller slid the last bottle of his recovered cargo into its cradle when the phone in the bookstore above him started ringing. He folded his arms across his chest and surveyed his replenished wine cellar. Smiling, he flipped the light switch off and bounded up the stairs.

"Headlands Bookstore," he said when he finally reached the phone at the front of the store. *Really need another extension.*

"Mr. Miller?"

"Yes?"

"Officer Crawford of the California Highway Patrol."

"Oh, hello. Did you ever find that car?" Tom trapped the cordless phone between his ear and shoulder, poured himself another cup of coffee, and headed for the reading corner, where he plopped down into his overstuffed chair.

"Yes, actually, we did. It apparently made it as far as the roundabout just south of Fort Bragg."

"And the driver?"

"We found her as well."

"Her?"

"Yes. An..." Tom could hear the officer leafing through the pages of what he assumed to be his notebook. "...Debra Osborn."

Tom, who was in the middle of taking a sip of coffee, slopped it into his lap. "Dammit!" he exclaimed, leaping to his feet and brushing the hot liquid from the front of his pants.

"Excuse me?"

"Huh? Oh sorry, just spilt my coffee is all. Did you say Debra Osborn?" He sat back down.

"That's right." More flipping of pages. "Apparently, she's from Los Angeles and has been missing for over two weeks."

"Two weeks? Missing from where?"

"Silver Lake Medical Center where she has been receiving treatment in one of their behavioral health programs for a bipolar disorder. Do you, by any chance, know this woman?"

Tom's gut reaction was to deny he'd ever set eyes on Debra but realized that could look bad. "Yes, unfortunately, I do."

"I suspected as much from what she was saying, although I'm not sure how much of it makes any sense."

"How's that?"

"Well, um..." Tom sensed something more than just hesitation. "The things she was saying seemed jumbled, almost incoherent."

"Really? What exactly did she say?"

"Well, she kept asking why the potion didn't work. Claims to have sent it to 'him' along with her reason. I assume she meant you. Any of this mean anything?"

"No, not a thing." Tom had suspected Debra was a bit off but this was crazy. He thanked the officer for calling, disconnected and moved over to his computer behind the counter. After opening the browser, he googled bipolar disorder.

"This condition can cause severe mood shifts from manic highs to deep depression," he read. "It can cause racing thoughts, reckless behaviors, and fast driving.

However, with consistent doctor's care, this mental illness can be treated." *Mental illness?* Scrolling down the page he found a section on treatment. "Medications include mood stabilizers, antipsychotics, and antidepressants. The most common treatment is lithium." Clicking on the search window, he typed in lithium. "Widely used in a variety of things including batteries, Pyrex cookware, lubricants, cosmetics, and plastics." He scrolled down until something caught his eye. "Lithium produces a bright pink flame when burned." He sat, staring at the screen. *Pink flame?* "The wine!" he exclaimed, slamming his hand down on the desk. "That damn bottle of wine I got must've come from Debra, and she put her lithium in it." *But how can I prove it?*

He grabbed his keys and quickly left the bookstore, locking the door behind him. Mounting the stairs to his apartment two at a time, he let himself in and began rummaging through the cupboard under the sink. "Aha!" he cried, pulling out the empty wine bottle with the yellow carnation on the label. "I thought I'd saved it." He pulled out the cork he'd hurriedly replaced that night on the beach and took a small sniff. The smell of cloves assaulted his nostrils. Tipping the bottle slightly, he held it up to the light. A few drops of the hideous liquid had remained inside. *Hopefully, enough to prove my theory.* He left the bottle on the counter and went back down to the bookstore. After locating Officer Crawford's business card and punching in his number, Tom googled one last thing — yellow carnations. He clicked on a link that showed multiple colors of carnations and what each meant. He'd just scrolled down to the yellow one when the phone call went though.

"Crawford."

Tom read the short paragraph.

"Hello?"

"Rejection, contempt, scorn..."

"Who is this?" Officer Crawford demanded.

Tom suddenly realized someone was speaking to him. "Oh, I'm sorry. This is Tom Miller."

"Yes, Mr. Miller. What can I do for you?"

"I think I've figured out what Debra was talking about." He explained about the emails she had sent him and the bottle of wine he'd received. "I still have it, and I'll be willing to bet it's laced with lithium as well as other substances." He agreed to turn it over to the highway patrolman the next time he passed by Mendocino.

After hanging up, Tom checked his watch. An hour to closing time, but he didn't care. He needed some kind of pastry right away, so he did a quick check of the store, flipped the sign around as he locked the door, and headed for the bed & breakfast. *Paul is not going to believe this!*

Beth Braddock was amazed summer was almost over, and the day she had worked so hard for was finally here. Each day, more and more people poured into Mendocino, and she and Paul had been very busy at the bed & breakfast. Any spare moment he had was spent helping Beth get ready for the show, and Suzy over at the art gallery, had let them use one of the smaller rooms to prepare and store her photos. Amy had ordered all of her enlargements, selling them to her at cost, and Tom had helped with the publicity. All that was left to do was show up and play the part of "artiste."

She pulled the lacy white dress she'd found in a little boutique in Fort Bragg over her head and smoothed it into place. Looking at her reflection, she was pleased to see it set off her sun-kissed skin and highlighted hair perfectly.

"I just hope those friends of mine don't expect me to go on tour," she said, smiling at Annie as she slipped on the white sandals Amy had insisted she borrow.

The chocolate lab panted her reply as she watched from her usual spot on the bed.

"I wish Tony and Steve could have come down," Beth continued as she stepped into the bathroom to apply what little make-up she'd planned to wear. "It just seemed so odd that neither of them could get away for the weekend."

After giving her hair one last spritz of hairspray, she grabbed the small designer backpack she'd also purchased at the boutique and slid one strap onto her shoulder. "Come on, girl. Time for you to go outside."

Annie followed her down the front steps and started toward the gate. "No you don't," Beth scolded. "You have to stay home." The old dog, her tongue moving in and out of her open mouth with each breath, looked over her shoulder at her owner. "Do I need to chain you up or will you just go lie down like a good girl?" Closing her mouth, Annie hung her head, moseyed over to her favorite spot at the foot of the stairs, and plopped down.

"See, that wasn't so hard," Beth said, reaching down and scratching her companion's ears. "You take a nap, and I'll be home before you know it." Then she latched the gate behind her, rounded the corner, and headed up Heeser Drive.

Paul Hayden checked his watch again. *If they don't get here soon, the surprise will be ruined.*

"Do you see her yet?" Amy asked as she joined him at his vantage point on the sidewalk in front of the Mendocino Art Center.

"No, not yet."

"I still don't know why you didn't just go pick her up."

Paul frowned at her. "Believe me I tried, but she insisted on walking here herself. Something about starting her new journey on her own." He turned around and looked toward Highway 1. "No sign of Tom either?"

Amy shook her head. "And I told him to get here as soon as he could because I figured the timing was gonna be close."

"Maybe the plane got delayed somehow." He shaded his eyes with one hand as he again looked down the hill. "Surprise or not, she'll be glad he came."

"Oh I think it'll be a surprise," Amy said, pointing back toward Lansing Street. "They're here."

A black Mazda MX-5 Miata pulled to the curb, and Tom stepped out.

"About time," Amy declared, placing her hands on her hips. "Where on earth have you been?"

"Relax. Just gave Tony here a little extra spin in my new car," he said, motioning toward the man climbing out on the passenger side.

"Beth is due here any moment," Amy continued, "and you two go on a joyride!"

"Whoa, hang on there." Tony held up both hands. "Wasn't my idea."

"Well, you're lucky she hasn't arrived yet."

Tom smiled. "So we're good, then."

Before Amy had a chance to reply, a loud screeching of tires got everyone's attention, and the four of them looked toward the hill but saw nothing.

Paul noticed a man who had been jogging toward them stop and turn around. "What's going on?" he called to him, stepping off the curb and leaving the others on the sidewalk.

"Can't really tell," the man yelled back. "Looks like maybe someone got hit."

An overwhelming sense of déjà vu gripped Paul. "No, no, no! This can't be happening!" He took off running and zipped past the jogger. Further down the hill, he saw an older white car in the middle of the road with its drivers side door hanging open. Several people had gathered around and were looking at something in front of it. "Please don't be Beth, please don't be Beth," he whispered over and over as he continued to run toward the commotion. Skidding to a stop, he was relieved to see Beth kneeling on the ground rather than lying on it.

She glanced at him, tear trails running down her face. "Oh Paul," she exclaimed, "it's Annie!"

"Lady, I'm so sorry." A man Paul guessed to be in his sixties stood near the front left fender, wringing his hands. "As soon as I spotted the dog coming across the road, I slammed on my brakes." He shook his head. "I didn't even think I hit it, 'til I seen you dash over."

Paul knelt down next to Beth. He felt bad that he hadn't even noticed the chocolate lab until Beth had said something. He laid his hand on the dog's side. "Well, she's breathing okay. Any sign of an injury?"

"Not that I've noticed but she's not moving."

"You want me to pick her up and carry her home?" Paul offered.

"Do you think we should...?" The old dog opened her eyes and raised her head. "Annie!" Then she struggled to her feet and shook her head.

Paul stood and helped Beth up. "She looks okay," he said, rubbing his hands along her sides and down each leg. "I'm guessing she got knocked out, hitting her head on that bumper."

"I'm so glad I didn't hurt your dog," the older man said, holding out his hand.

"I think she'll be fine," Paul said, shaking hands. *Thank goodness!* He didn't want anything to spoil this day for Beth.

"She's always been a lucky dog."

"Tony!" Beth threw her arms around her brother-in-law's neck, and he picked her up as he hugged her.

"Hello, Beautiful," he said, setting her down.

"What are you doing here?"

"A friend of yours invited me to your showing." He grinned at Paul.

"And I'm glad he did." Beth looked at each man in turn. "That way I can have both of my favorite guys share this with me."

As the three of them moved over to the side of the road, Paul wrapped his arm around Beth's waist and held her close. She smiled up at him, but as soon as their eyes met, her expression changed. "Are you all right?"

"I am now, and I'll explain it all to you, later. This day is all about you, and I want you to enjoy it."

"Come on you two," Tony said, starting back up the hill toward the gallery. "We better get a move on. I'm sure the others are anxiously waiting."

"Waiting for what?" Beth asked.

Paul and Tony exchanged glances over the top of her head. "For you," they said in unison and then laughed.

"Oh yeah, right." She giggled. "I'd almost forgotten."

Still feeling slightly nervous, Beth Braddock stared at her reflection in the mirror over the sink in the tiny unisex bathroom at the back of the gallery, her chance to slip out the back door long gone. Everyone, including Annie, was waiting for her to appear so they could tell her how wonderful her photographs were. And they were too, thanks to Paul. But that wasn't all he had helped her with; he had shown her she could love again, and for that she would forever be grateful.

EPILOGUE

"We'd also like a pitcher of margaritas and some taquitos and guacamole," Paul told the waitress, handing over his menu.

"You remembered," Amy said, surrendering hers as well.

"How could I forget. Last time we were here, Tom almost choked to death on one. Didn't you, buddy?" Paul clapped him on the back a couple of times.

Tom glared at him. "You're not nearly as funny as you think you are, you know. That woman tried to kill me!"

"Sure I am. You just haven't realized it yet. And it was only a near miss. You're still here and she's locked up, right?"

"For now," Tom muttered.

Before Paul could say anything more, the waitress returned carrying a frosty pitcher of margaritas and a tray with four salt-rimmed glasses.

"Would you do the honors?" Beth asked, holding her glass toward Tom.

"Absolutely." One by one, he filled the glasses with the pale green, frozen beverage.

"Mmmm, that hits the spot," Amy declared. She set her glass down and grabbed one of the taquitos that had just been delivered to the table. "So how's the training going?" she asked Beth as she twirled it in guacamole that had been mounded in the center of the large platter.

"What training?" Tom asked.

"Clara's retiring," Paul said, snagging his own taquito. "She and Gladys are going to do some traveling."

"Retiring? She can't retire!" Tom's voice got louder. "Who's going make all those wonderful pastries?"

"Calm down," Amy scolded. "You're causing a scene."

"Okay, okay — sorry. But please tell me she's still going to do some baking."

Beth and Paul looked at each other and grinned. "That's what the training is for," Beth said, patting Tom's hand. "I'm going to learn how to make all those wonderful goodies." She winked at Paul. "Maybe we'll even have maple nut scones more often than once a year."

"Really?" Tom exclaimed. "That would be great!" The other three looked at him and burst out laughing.

"You are a mess Tom Miller," Amy told him.

"And you should know Amy Miller," he retorted.

"That still sounds kinda strange," Amy admitted, reaching for her fourth taquito.

"What's even stranger is having to drive to work again." Tom picked up the pitcher and refilled everyone's glass. "Really hated leaving my new furniture behind too, but..." He looked at Paul. "...it doesn't quite fit with the rest of the décor."

"Exactly!" he chuckled. "So what are you going to do with your apartment above the bookstore?"

"Well, I haven't decided completely, but I put out a few 'feelers' and I think I'm going to offer it as an exclusive writers' retreat. Come to Mendocino and get inspired," he said, swiping his hand through the air over his head.

"Catchy," Paul said. Then he looked at Beth. "That might work for your house."

She frowned at him. "Make it a writers' retreat?"

"No, but I could offer it as a long term rental option through the bed & breakfast. Leave it furnished and rent it by the week."

"But where will you live?" Amy asked her friend.

Paul's smile faded from his face as he turned toward Amy. "Beth is moving."

"You're moving?" Beth lowered her head and nodded. "Where?" Amy demanded.

Slowly, she met Amy's gaze. "Paul's" she whispered.

"Really?" Amy shrieked. Beth smiled and nodded again.

Tom leaned over closer to his wife. "Uh, now you're making a scene."

"Oh stop it," she said, smacking his arm loud enough to attract the attention of the diners at the next table. "That's wonderful." Suddenly the expression on her face changed. "What's Tony gonna say about it? He might think you should get married first."

"Don't see why," Tom said as he focused on selecting the perfect taquito. "He's living with someone he's not married to, isn't he?" After a few moments of silence, he looked up to find three pairs of eyes staring at him. "What?"

Amy spoke first. "Tom Miller, sometimes you are the most exasperating pompous..."

"I'd like to propose a toast," Paul interrupted. "Here's to a wonderful place to live and goods friends to be with."

"To good friends," the other three echoed in unison, clinking their glasses against Paul's.

"Now let's eat," Amy said, clapping her hands as the waitress lowered the large serving tray onto a stand she'd brought along. "I'm starving!"

www.ingramcontent.com/pod-product-compliance
Lightning Source LLC
Chambersburg PA
CBHW032141020726
47496CB00003B/662